Also by Teresa Collard

Published by Severn House Ltd:
Murder at the Tower
Murder at the Royal Shakespeare Th.
Murder at Hampton Court Palace

Published by First Century
The Sun Should Never Shine
But for the Grace of God

After leaving RADA, Teresa Collard has spent her life involved in the Arts. She was the first administrator at the Swan Theatre, Worcester then on to Questers Theatre, Ealing. She was the first manager at the Neptune theatre, Liverpool, where she established the Neptune Theatre Company and ran art exhibitions. It was there that a love for children's entertainment developed. She wrote and directed children's plays and documentaries before going on to run the Bluecoat Art Gallery in Liverpool. After Liverpool she became Arts and Entertainment Manager for the Borough of Milton Keynes. A notable achievement was the highly acclaimed February Festival (1977 – 1983). Together with the composer David Lyon she developed performances for children based on history, in which the audience were totally involved, starting with the nationally acclaimed Battle of Trafalgar. Later they produced Charter Extravaganza, based on the history of Northamptonshire, which was performed in Northampton and at The Albert Hall. In the 1980s she moved to the village of Hanwell in Oxfordshire, where she began writing murder mysteries.

ISBN 978-1-4717-4782-3

THE BASKERVILLE

INHERITANCE

Reminiscences of John H. Watson M.D.

Teresa Collard

Acknowledgements

Many years ago, being a Sherlock Holmes aficionado, I wrote a sequel to Conan Doyle's Hound of the Baskervilles. Unfortunately my lovely agent, Rosemary, left this planet, so the story was never published. Now nearing my ninth decade, and my sight not being as it should be, I decided to self-publish. I have relied upon my granddaughter's magical dexterity in designing and publishing the book and also my friend Lynda Zachary and my Grandson Daniel who spent untold hours editing. Many thanks to Elizabeth and Daniel Baines and Lynda Zachary for their dedication.

CHAPTER ONE

Holmes sat with his uneaten breakfast in front of him, staring into space. Normally I knew the signs only too well, but it was something deeper than his usual ennui, something I simply could not fathom. Maybe he was, of course, suffering from two weeks inactivity, but that did not explain his total lack of appetite. Peering at him through a maze of shag tobacco smoke thicker than any London smog, I asked him why he was so despondent.

'Stagnation, Watson, is a state to be avoided. Give me an equation to solve, or a formidable and demanding cipher to decode; release me from this unvarying run of hour after hour of depression, for it is anathema to me.'

'Boredom, Holmes,' I said, provoked beyond my normal long-suffering endurance, 'would be easy to ameliorate by reading a couple of the latest biographies.'

'You know full well, Watson,' he snorted, 'that I have no deep interest in any subject that has no direct bearing upon that pursuit which I have made my life's sole purpose. I must tell you that you too, are suffering the effects of this appalling weather. No need to look at me in astonishment. You never complain about your rheumatism, but it is perfectly obvious to me that in wet weather, when particularly prolonged, you suffer the effects of your injuries inflicted by the enemy at Maiwand.'

'For once, Holmes, you are wrong. Of course the damp weather occasionally exacerbates the condition, but it reminds

1

me, forcibly, that I am lucky to be alive. To see one's comrades slaughtered and to survive a massacre is a salutary reminder of how fate controls our destinies.'

'Ah, that is where you are mistaken, Watson. You must concede, my dear fellow, that I am in fact, correct in my judgement. You are in some considerable physical discomfort.' I murmured my reluctant assent as he continued on a different tack.

'We control our own destinies, with help from our friends, and frequently our enemies. Our knowledge is indeed limited, but the frontiers roll back daily. Oh Watson, what have you learned from our great experiences? Nothing? Where has "fate" played a hand? Would not "fate" have destroyed Sir Henry Baskerville, but for our timely intervention in thwarting the assassin, but why did I allow Stapleton to escape justice?'

Again and again Holmes had mentioned the Baskerville affair. But why? Never had any other case so obsessed him. Now I knew what was on my friend's mind. His success in solving the crime was marred by the fact that a villainous man had escaped. For Holmes this was tantamount to failure.

At the time he assumed, as I did, that this brutish man who had trained a hound to kill and who had beaten his wife black and blue before tying her to a pillar, had been sucked into Grimpen Mire. On the night he fled there had been a thick fog and his wife, whom we rescued, told us he would make his way to an old tin mine on an island in the heart of the Mire. It was evident that pursuit would be in vain until the fog lifted. When, eventually, we were able to make our way to the mine, there was no trace of the man. We assumed he had missed his footing and had sunk without trace.

Mrs Hudson bustled in. She took one look at the cold, congealed food on my companion's plate, shook her head, frowned, and removed the inedible bacon, egg and kidney. 'I had better cook you another breakfast, Mr Holmes.'
'Just a piece of toast, Mrs Hudson, my appetite has abated.'
Mrs Hudson turned to leave, glowering, tut-tutting, and muttering something under her breath.

'My dear Mrs Hudson, you forget yourself!'

I took this for a mild reproach, as I am sure Mrs H did, for she stopped in her tracks and looked at Holmes with an apologetic expression.

'I didn't mean to offend, Mr Holmes, but there's those who would have loved...'

'No no, Mrs Hudson, your rebuke is well taken, and well deserved. You came up here to announce a visitor, did you not?' She nodded. Holmes elaborated 'It is a common man, a workman of some sort; he is dirty, and obviously in a hurry.'

Holmes enjoyed greatly this baiting, and I must confess, though I myself was often at the butt end of it, I enjoyed it too. No doubt these conclusions of his were entirely logical and correct!

'Why, yes, Mr Holmes. I came up to tell you, sir, that there is a truly disreputable person at the door. But how could you have known?'

'No surprises, I am afraid, eh Watson?'

'None. I also heard the bell.'

Holmes laughed. 'In this tedious nothingness, the slightest sound travels. And I can see from your demeanour, Mrs Hudson, that you disapprove. My experience has led me to understand your sometimes less than charitable nature towards the least fortunate classes of our society. My breakfast, or lack of it, took preference over a poor man who is waiting outside. Unforgivable, I must say, in this rain. I can only deduce that you do not wish him to foul your immaculately clean hallway and stairs.'

I chuckled, although there was no sign of levity on Holmes's face. Mrs Hudson, still not quite following my friend's drift, asked, 'Shall I have him wait outside while I make you some fresh toast?'

'Outside in this rain! Never! Show him in, Mrs Hudson, and do nothing about the toast. It is of little consequence.'

An amazing metamorphosis took place. My companion's lethargy vanished, he sat up, alert, eyes sparkling, and the tips of his fingers met as though in prayer. The visitor, not waiting to be announced, rushed in without a 'by your leave', out of breath and smelling horribly. Holmes closed his eyes and took a deep breath, as though savouring a most exotic perfume.

'Sir, sir,' gasped the visitor, who was red in the face with sweat pouring off him, with curious black smudges on the side of his face.

'Take your time, man,' said Holmes, 'for unless you get your breath back you will not be able to impart your news.' The frightened man dashed to the window, looked down on Baker Street, then turned to Holmes with a mute appeal.

'All right, first of all tell me your name.'

'Charley, sir, Charley Mayne.'

'Good. Secondly, why have you come to me, thirdly, from whom, precisely, are you escaping, and fourthly, what has a chimney sweep done to become involved with the law?' The poor man looked bewildered. 'You have little time to explain, so perhaps you had better get on with it.'

'I come to you, sir, because you're the only person I knows can 'elp. I sweep the chimneys for Mr Wilson at the Express Office and I've often 'eard 'im telling 'is reporters to keep tabs on you, sir. 'Ee says you're good news.'

Holmes nodded his agreement. 'Now where did the police arrest you?'

'Outside Ted Miller's place. He's my mate.'

'Ted Miller,' mused Holmes. 'Are we talking about the well-known amateur wrestler?'

'Yes, sir.'

'You had better tell me, Charley, exactly what you have done.'
'I aint done nothing, but my mate was found dead in his own back yard. Ted had been strangled, and the coppers think I did it.'

'You had better tell me the truth. Did you?'

'Cross me 'eart, and 'ope to die, I never touched 'im.'

'Why is it, Charley, that I have the feeling you know why he was murdered?'

'No, I don't, sir, not reelly. It don't make no sense.'

Let me be the judge of that.' Their conversation was interrupted by the sound of a cab arriving and a furious banging downstairs.

'Quick, Charley, out of the window and down the pipe.'

'But,' I intervened, 'he will break his neck.'

'Not a chimney sweep, Watson, they have the ability to climb like monkeys.'

Holmes quickly turned his attention to Charley. 'Do you know the *Empress of India* near the Express Office?'

'Yes, sir.

'Meet me there in an hour's time.'

With considerable misgivings, I opened the window and let the panic-stricken man escape. I thought Holmes was making a mistake. This time the law had to be right. I watched as Charley dexterously negotiated his descent in less time than it took Lestrade to climb the stairs.

'Good-morning Inspector,' said Holmes, in an unusually welcoming tone. Charley and his problems had dispelled the gloom and boredom that had affected my friend for the past two weeks.

'Where is he, Holmes?' shouted Lestrade. 'What have you done with him?'

'He was like quick silver, Lestrade, he simply leapt out of the window. There was no stopping him, it was a feat to be admired.' Holmes stood back from the open window, his face expressing true admiration.

Lestrade strode angrily to the window. 'Get after him,' he ordered the constable who was standing in the doorway. 'Escaping, Holmes, in my book says it all. He is guilty, guilty of murdering his partner, Ted Miller, in the early hours of this morning.'

'The victim was a small man, I take it?'

'Yes...well ... short.'

'How was the victim murdered?'

'Strangled with a cord.'

'Must have been quite a struggle,' mused Holmes. 'Two active, agile men of short stature, who were well matched. It is a mystery, Lestrade, is it not, how either man could dispose of his partner?'

'Are you saying it was manslaughter, not murder?

'At this stage I am saying nothing.'

Lestrade pushed his hat back on his head and scratched his scalp. 'Are you trying to suggest, Mr Holmes, that the felon who has just performed a vanishing trick from your window is not the murderer?'

'Motive, Lestrade. What motive would he have?'

'Had he not escaped I would be asking him the same question,' replied Lestrade angrily, 'but I have two witnesses, unimpeachable witnesses, who heard Charley Mayne and his mate Ted Miller having a fierce argument yesterday evening, almost coming to blows.'

'Witnesses?'

'The two boys employed by Mayne and Miller.'

'Oh unimpeachable, my dear Lestrade, I do agree! It would be an interesting exercise, Inspector, to enquire how often the two men quarrelled. It could have been a daily occurrence, or a contretemps that happened twice a week, when the adrenalin was flowing. If you will permit me, Inspector, to visit the scene of crime, and speak to the witnesses, then we would be some way to solving the crime.'

Lestrade and I looked at each other in astonishment, thinking that this time Holmes had lost his way. I put it down to the inactivity of the previous two weeks, and his preoccupation with the Baskerville case. The Inspector and I both believed Charley to be guilty. An argument followed, by near fisticuffs, said it all. Who else would have reason to murder a simple chimney sweep?

CHAPTER TWO

Whilst on our way to India Street to view the scene of the crime I thought about the events at Baskerville Hall some two years previously. At the time, local gossip had it that no man dared to cross the moor at night because there were reports of a gigantic hound whose blood curdling snarling had been heard many time upon the moor. Several men had mentioned seeing this Baskerville demon, and all agreed it was a vast creature, luminous, ghastly and spectral. Dr Mortimer, who, some four years since, had examined the corpse of Sir Charles Baskerville, admitted, despite being a man of science and a realist, that there might be some truth in the 17th century legend describing a hound that had torn out the throat of another, earlier, Baskerville. He was adamant that there had been no signs of violence, only an incredible facial distortion that could be ascribed to the shock of seeing a horrendous ghostly beast. Holmes made it clear that hitherto he had confined his investigations to this world, and would continue to do so. For him the death was not supernatural and could only be solved by deduction, not intuition.

There were, however, one or two spirited mortals who had dared to cross the moor at night. Selden, a wretched prisoner who had escaped from Dartmoor, preferred the freedom of the open countryside to incarceration for life in a gruesome prison, but he was not alone on the moor. Holmes, who had sent me to Baskerville Hall to keep a constant eye on Sir Henry, gave me to believe that he was remaining in London, but this was not the case.

One late afternoon, on seeing a tall, thin figure roaming the moor, I was determined to follow the fellow. At last I managed to get close enough to hear boots striking upon stone. With my pistol cocked I shrank back into a dark corner, only to be assailed by Holmes, who was amused to see me ready for action. Telling me to exercise caution with the revolver, he explained that he had adopted the role of a tourist, and in such guise, had discovered the identity of the murderer. For a few days he had bedded down in a cave, with sustenance being delivered by young Cartwright from the Express Office.

I have to say I was angry about the deception that had been practised, but Holmes was fulsome in his praise for the precautions I had taken to make sure Sir Henry was safe.

As we traipsed across the moor on our way back to the hall we heard a prolonged yell of utter horror, followed by desperate screams intermingled with a creature yowling.

'The hound!' yelled Holmes.

In fear and trepidation we ran towards the screaming man, but we were too late. Sir Henry lay prostrate upon a stone, face downwards. We recognised him by the clothes he was wearing. Holmes was like a man totally distraught, stamping his feet, wiping his forehead and whispering, 'We are too late.'

As I turned the body over, Holmes uttered a cry, almost of triumph, as he too bent over the corpse. The man who was bearded and filthy was not the baronet, but Selden, the escaped convict.

'Watson' Homes shouted, 'this mistake is our inheritance'. On hearing the hound yapping at his heels, Selden had obviously run for his life and crashed to his death on the rocks. Responding to Holmes, I vowed that I would rather inherit a gold mine.

'Not in this part of the world' retorted Holmes 'it would be a tin mine here'.

Moments later, Stapleton, a naturalist living at Merripit House on the Baskerville Estate, appeared on the scene. He took a close look at Selden, and even in the moonlight, we could see that, for a moment, he looked utterly bewildered.

Those few seconds proved to Holmes that he had indeed solved the murder of Sir Charles Baskerville, the attempted murder of Sir Henry and the death of a convict known as the Notting Hill murderer.

Selden's sister, wife of the butler at Baskerville Hall, had given her convict brother some of Sir Henry's old clothes and it was the scent of the garments that had attracted the hound. Ergo Sir Henry was the intended victim, not the wretched convict.

Prior to the death of Selden, Holmes had telegraphed Lestrade, expecting him to come down on the night train but the Inspector was delayed, and by the time he arrived Stapleton had escaped. There still remained the slight possibility that he had been sucked into Grimpen Mire but this was unlikely because he knew his way around the moor. Holmes, who was angry with himself for allowing the villain to escape, said he should have made his move earlier. Failure was unforgivable. Ah well, it doesn't do to dwell on the past.

On our return to Paddington we were held up for four hours, owing to the fact that there had been a murder on the train ahead. During the long wait Holmes strode up and down the corridor, venting his spleen. There was no doubt that he was still angry with himself but I knew our visit to the East End would occupy his mind for a few days.

India Street is a typical terraced East End Street. Two up, two down, with front doors abutting the pavement. At the rear of each house is a small, roughly paved yard in which the W.C. is situated, and egress from the yard is through a six-foot door that opened outwards on to an alley serving two streets. Lestrade led us straight through the front room, where a young woman sat sobbing, and out into the back yard, where a constable on duty was awaiting the arrival of the pathologist.

The corpse lay face downwards, with the means of execution still in place around his neck. A pick-axe and a bag lay beside the recumbent form of the dead chimney sweep. Holmes picked up the bag, looked carefully inside, and then, to our astonishment, put his head into the bag and sniffed. I must admit he looked for all the world like a donkey about to enjoy his oats, which caused Lestrade to chuckle audibly, which for some obscure reason annoyed me.

'The bag tells us nothing, Mr Holmes. It was merely the means of conveying the pickaxe and the rope to the scene-of-the-crime.'

Holmes shook his head. 'Not so, Lestrade, not so.' Carefully, he replaced the bag in its original position. 'You have ascertained, then,' said Holmes sharply, 'that the pickaxe, which is an important clue, was brought here by the murderer in that bag?'

'It's common sense,' growled the inspector, obviously annoyed at the attitude of my friend. 'No man would walk openly through the streets with the instruments of murder displayed for all to see. It's quite obvious to me that Charley Mayne decided to assassinate his partner with a pickaxe.'

'Why then,' enquired Holmes mildly, 'did he change his mind and use the rope? And how is it that Charley, a small man, only 5' 3" in height, managed to strangle his partner, who had some status as an amateur wrestler?'

Lestrade had no answer, and watched as Holmes, with his curious, loping stride, walked backwards and forwards in that small back yard, sniffing. He stopped abruptly at the remains of a fire, knelt down, sniffed again, and remained there with his eyes closed. Had I not known my friend so well I might have easily mistaken him for a devout advocate of an Eastern faith, at his devotions. For a few seconds my thoughts returned to India where, when the muezzin calls, all good Moslems face Mecca, fall on their knees and pray.

Suddenly Holmes leapt to his feet, consulted his watch, nodded his head several times, then looked at me with a mischievous grin.

'Well Watson, you of all people should know what has been happening here.'

My friend, with his unerring instinct for deduction, had, from that wretched scene in a backyard, drawn conclusions, but why should I have known what had happened?

'All I know, Holmes, is that we have the corpse of a man who has been strangled. The murderer's first intent may have been to use the pickaxe. It would have been possible last night because there was a full moon, but supposing, at the last moment, cloud cover thwarted his intentions, prevented him from seeing his victim clearly, which meant he had to use the rope, and creeping up behind the poor unsuspecting man, strangle him?'

Holmes gave a snort. 'You disappoint me, Watson. Of all cases we have investigated together, this one should have been your case. Now, with the Inspector's permission, turn the victim over and let us see if he was a poor unsuspecting fool.'

Lestrade, still annoyed at losing his suspect, bent his head in a gesture of assent, and together we turned the corpse over while Holmes, humming to himself, observed our efforts. As we did so, one of the dead man's shoes fell off. Holmes retrieved it, and for some inexplicable reason slipped his hand into the shoe before replacing it beside the victim.

'Good God!' said Lestrade, as we gazed down on Ted Miller, whose expression was utterly spine-chilling, 'he wasn't taken unawares, he knew what was happening.'

'You are right,' said Holmes, 'this was no surprise killing. This was an execution. Now, if you will excuse me, Inspector, I have an appointment a stone's throw from here, in less than ten minutes. Let me know the findings of your pathologist. They will, I am sure, make interesting reading. Come on, Watson, we must not delay. A man's life is at stake.'

We left the house, hoping to pick up a cab immediately, and I was astonished when Holmes stopped suddenly and put up his umbrella, despite the fact that the skies were clear and blue.

'It is my only cover, Watson, but you must make haste and discover the identity of that elegant lady ahead of us who is heading towards a waiting coach. We must know what interests a lady of quality enough to bring her to this poverty-stricken part of the world.'

I lost no time in following the lady, who was dressed in a red velvet gown and richly decorated shawl. She quickened her steps as though she knew I was there but never once turned round. She was swiftly assisted in boarding the coach by one of the grooms, but before the carriage moved away, she looked down at me and smiled. Not a young woman, but a beautiful woman, in whose enigmatic smile there was confidence, and a hint of amusement at my gauche show of interest. As the carriage turned the corner I had the satisfaction of seeing a crest emblazoned on its door. Three fleurs de lis, a lion couchant and the motto *celer et audax*. The lady would not be too difficult to trace.

Holmes seemed quite satisfied. *'Celer et audax,'* he muttered. 'Speed and audacity, Watson, a good motto, which we must observe this very moment.'

Holmes, as I knew only too well, by the set of his jaw, the light in his eye and a slight smile which registered mental satisfaction, was already well on the way to solving the crime. I had no such satisfaction.

'Well, Holmes, what do you make of it?'

'Watson, it is you who have lived in India who should be telling me what happened. Think, my friend, think. Which religious sect in India has rigidly preserved rites in which a pickaxe and the sacrifice of sugar form a part? Which sect traces its origins to seven Mohammedan tribes, proscribed by Islam, but which flourished until Lord Bentinck took vigorous action in outlawing the system, and which sect garrotted its victims?'

'You are describing Thuggeeism, Holmes, which is now extinct.'

'Not, I think, totally, for if you care to read the *Thuggee and Dacoity Report* of 1879 you will find the number of registered Punjabi and Hindustani Thugs still numbered 344.'

'That smell, Holmes, that curious smell was caramel, none other than burnt sugar.'

Holmes stopped in his headlong race towards *The Empress of India* and slapped me on the back.

17

'At last, Watson, at last you have made the connection.'

When we arrived we had to push our way through a writhing mass of seafarers from all corners of the globe. We found Charley tucked away in a corner with the dregs of a glass of ale and the remains of six oysters. There was scarcely room for a dwarf, and conversation would have been impossible under such conditions. Charley recognised our dilemma. 'I'll come outside, Mr Holmes.'

'No, you stay where you are, Charley,' ordered Holmes, 'while Dr Watson enquires from the proprietor whether there is a private room available.'

'How long do you want it for, luvvy?' asked the buxom, red headed Mrs White. 'It aint cheap, you know.'

'No more than an hour. We need to talk to a client.'

'Oh, solicitors, are you?'

'Not exactly. I am a doctor, and my friend is a detective.'

'You're not doing down one of my customers, are you?'

'Nothing could be further from our thoughts, Madam. Mr Holmes, I am sure, will be protecting his interests.'

'What! You don't say that the famous Sherlock Holmes is actually in my pub?'

'Hush, Madam, please keep your voice down.'

'Here doctor,' she said with a stage whisper that would have filled *The Gaiety*. You and Mr Holmes can use my private sitting room. I'll not charge you.'

'That is most kind, madam.'

Excited, Mrs White ran across the room to Holmes, and winked at him. To my utter surprise, he returned the wink.
'Here, you follow me, sir.'

Her sitting room was only large enough to accommodate a sofa and one easy chair. The antimacassars were thick with oil and the red curtains, blowing slightly in the breeze, exuded a distinct smell of stale beer.

'This all right, sir?' asked Mrs White, looking anxiously at Holmes.

'Excellent, my dear Mrs White.'

'Sir,' she was a little hesitant, 'would you let me have a signed photograph? It would look good in the bar.'

Holmes smiled down at her, and like a distinguished thespian, thrived on her adulation. It has crossed my mind many, many times that Holmes would have made an excellent actor, with his love of assuming disguises and the ineffable ease with which he projects his voice.

'Of course you shall have a photograph, and it shall be signed, but now dear lady, if you could leave us in peace?'

'Of course, sir, of course.' She very nearly dropped him a full curtsey, surprising us all, before bustling from the room.

'Now, Watson, close the window. We don't know who is hanging around, and who may be listening.'

'You don't mean the coppers have followed you 'ere?' asked Charley fearfully.

'No, but it would be immeasurably better for you had they done so.'

'Are you saying, guv, that I did it?'

No, Charley, this was hardly the crime of one man, and with certainty I can say it was not committed by an Englishman, but before moving another finger to help you I must hear the truth.'

'The truth?' Charley whispered.

'Yes,' said Holmes. 'We have very little time, and for your own safety I advise you to tell me exactly what happened yesterday from the time you started work until the time you finished.'

'All right, guv, all right. We get up at 5 o'clock, that's me and my wife Liza. We have a bowl of porridge, then off she goes to the Bank of England, where she has a responsible cleaning job. When she 'as gone I get the cart wiv all me brushes on it, out of the backyard, and wait for Ted and the two lads to arrive. Yesterday we left my place at 5.30 on the dot 'cos we was working in the toff's end of town, and it's a fair old walk, but it pays better up there, so wot you loses on the roundabouts you gains on the swings. Jimmy and Mick have been with us now for nearly eighteen months. They're both twelve years old, but Mick has shot up the last few weeks and we'll 'ave to replace 'im. We walked along.... _ '

'All right, all right,' said Holmes impatiently, 'there is no need to describe the route you took. All I need to know is where you worked, whose houses, and the time.'

'The 'ouses yesterday were all in Belgrave Square. Big 'ouses with several fireplaces, so it takes us a day to go through the lot. We do them properly, give em a right going over. Don't want to lose these jobs cos the rhino's right. There's three 'ouses next to each other on the north side. At the first one the owners was away in France, on the riveera, the cook said, not that we ever see the owners, it's an 'igh and mighty butler who tells us wot to do.

We finished the first 'ouse at 9 o'clock. I know it was 9 cos I 'eard Big Ben striking the hour. The second 'ouse didn't take long because the old man 'ad died and they'd not lit any fires in 'is study or 'is bedroom. At the third 'ouse, *Altair* it's called, funny name that, we took much longer than usual because everything was at sixes and sevens. They 'ad forgotten we were coming and 'adn't put down druggets on the floor or covered the furniture. We carry our own, you understand, but we always lay ours round the fireplace.'

'You can stop there for a moment,' said Holmes, with his attention firmly fixed on a black and white picture of our Queen, though I'll guarantee he didn't see a single line of the drawing. '*Altair*,' he said at last, 'I believe is the residence of Lady Loubes-Bernac. Is that not so?'

'Yes, sir.'

'Now then, Charley, describe the pictures and the carpets.'

'There wasn't much time sir so I didn't take any notice.'

'Come now,' said Holmes sharply, 'you must have observed something. Were the carpets all white, or all blue?'

'No, they wasn't white, several sorts of big rugs, sort of oriental like.'

'Good. And on the walls I expect all the pictures were of quiet pastoral scenes.'

Charley looked bemused. 'Scenes of the countryside,' I explained.

'Oh no, they weren't pictures of places, they were paintings of people, army people, all looking straight at me, and a sort of shield thing with a lion lying down, and some sort of blue and gold decoration over its 'ed, and there was a sort of pattern of swords.'

'What an excellent collective noun, Watson, a pattern of swords, and how excellently Charley has described the room. Well done, Charley, well done. You have also solved a puzzle. We know a coach displaying the shield you describe was making for Belgrave Square. Now, how about the luxurious armchairs, sofas and tables?'

'They looked ordinary, like we see in any toff's 'ouse, except for ....'

'Yes?'

'Except for some small tables made of bamboo.'

'Excellent. We will make a competent observer of you, yet. You see, Charley all you had to do was concentrate. Now I need a full description of how you utilised your time in Lady Loubes-Bernac's house, and Charley, the truth please.'

The chimney sweep, who appeared to get smaller and smaller, looked at us both warily. It was obvious to me that Holmes already knew what had happened at *Altair*, but confirmation from this unhappy man would make him doubly sure.

'Ted and Mick worked one side of the 'ouse, while Jimmy and I did the other. We started in the kitchen which is the most difficult because of the big range, not only that, we like to get the worst over first, the smell of curry always hanging about fair makes your stomach 'eave. When we'd finished in the kitchen we did the nursery, and after that the sitting room. It 'as a big chimney which Jimmy shins up with no bother. I stepped into the chimney to give 'im the brushes, but as I put my 'and on a ledge to steady myself I felt summat move. Sounded like metal, so I yelled to Jimmy to wait while I took a decko. It was one of those metal cash boxes with the key still in it. Naturally, guv, I unlocked it, 'ad to didn't I, and you could have knocked me down with a fevver, because it was full of sparkling red stones.'

'So what did you do, Charley?'

'Well,' he said looking at the floor, 'I locked it up and put it back on the ledge.'

'The truth, Charley.'

'It's true, cross my heart. I locked it up and put it back.'

'But not,' said Holmes, 'before you had helped yourself.' Holmes opened his hand and there, in his palm, lay an exquisite ruby. 'How many did you take, Charley?'

'Two,' he whispered.

'That was my thinking. One for you and one for your deceased partner which he hid in his shoe.'

The chastened chimney sweep put his hand in his pocket and produced another ruby even larger and more glittering than the one Holmes was holding.

'Watson,' said Holmes as he took the ruby from Charley's grasp, 'you take care of these two priceless gems. It will be

24

safer for Charley not to have the fruits of larceny on his person.'

'Now before you give yourself up, my friend, let me hazard a guess at why you and your partner nearly came to blows early yesterday evening.'

'Give myself up?' Charley's voice was no more than a squeak. 'You don't mean that Mr Holmes? I never done it, truly I never done it.'

'It is patently obvious that the only crime you have committed is the abstraction of two precious stones from a house in Belgrave Square. The rubies you will return, via the good services of Inspector Lestrade, but not until I have solved the case and have seen the assassins arrested. Now let me get back to the row which developed between you and your partner.'

'He was angry because I didn't let on about the rubies until the end of the day. I 'id 'em, didn't tell Jimmy and Mick, you know what young lads are like, all mouth and no sense. Ted was furious because I didna take the whole box, said we would never 'ave 'ad to work again if I 'adn't been so lily-livered.'

Holmes smiled slightly. 'You have confirmed my hypothesis.'
'You aint going to turn me in, are you Mr Holmes?'

'Yes, Charley, because if I fail to hand you over into Inspector Lestrade's care, you will, by sunset today, also be a corpse. Doctor Watson will take a cab to your home and advise your wife to stay with friends or relatives for the next three days, and by the end of the third day I will have solved the case.

You must trust me.'

Charley Mayne's expression said it all. Prison for him, at that moment, meant a life sentence.

CHAPTER THREE

While on my way to see Mrs Mayne I gave some thought to the assassins who were out for Charley's blood. Not English, Holmes had said. Nevertheless, no one commits murder for the sake of two rubies and why would any sane person secrete precious stones in a chimney that was in constant use. Suddenly I remembered Holmes' dictum, *Look for the unusual in a case, Watson, and all will be revealed.*

Mrs Mayne, a fair-haired, pretty woman of some thirty summers, led me into the front room, which was immaculate, a fact which made me certain she never allowed Charley across the threshold until he had scrubbed himself raw and eradicated all signs of his day's endeavours. She was blissfully unaware that Ted had been murdered or that Charley was wanted by the police, but like a messenger of doom, I had to break the news. Shrieking like a wounded animal, she fainted clean away. I laid her on the sofa, then soaked a cloth in water and wiped her brow.

Liza Mayne was essentially a sensible woman, it was not too difficult to make her understand that both she and Charley were in danger. Her husband, I told her, was being given sanctuary in a police cell and it would be advisable if she would allow me to order a cab and take her to relatives or friends where she would be safe. Making no bones about packing her bag, she allowed me to escort her to her mother's house in Battersea. Before leaving, however, I peered through the windows from behind the lace curtains in case anyone was watching the house. My problem, and I blame Holmes for this, was that I had no idea who might be lurking. I was about to say the coast was clear when I caught a glimpse of a slight movement behind a nearby cart.

'There's someone out there,' I said to Mrs Mayne, 'someone behind that cart.' As I watched, the figure of a young lad crept round the vehicle. I am hardly clairvoyant, but it came to me in an instant, that the lad standing immobile beside the cart, eyeing the house, was one of the young sweeps employed by Charley. To give verisimilitude to my thoughts, he sped towards the front door. 'Quickly,' I said to Mrs Mayne, 'open the door, we have a visitor.' She was alert, I will say that for her. The door was ajar before our unexpected visitor had time to knock.

'Jimmy, what is the matter?'

'I 'av done summat awful, Mrs Mayne. They got me all mixed up, made me say things I 'adn't even thought abart, threatened me they did.'

'Who threatened you?'

27

As the door closed behind the frightened lad he turned and saw me. 'Cripes! Ee aint another one is ee? I'm orf.'

'No, Jimmy, no,' shouted Mrs Mayne as she put her foot against the door.

'Dr Watson is here to help us. Now you calm down, and come into the kitchen and tell us what it's all about.'

Despite the situation I had to smile, for Mrs Mayne had no intention of allowing Jimmy to enter her spotlessly clean front room. The back room was a doll's house of a kitchen. Hardly enough room for three people, and only two stools beside the table.

'Now you stand there, Jimmy, while I make a cup of tea for Dr Watson.'

'I never meant to do it. Honest, I never meant wot I said.'

Jimmy was on the verge of tears. 'They made me.'

'Who made you do what, Jimmy?' I asked quietly.

'It was them coppers, sir. They kept askin, and askin, and 'ollerin at me, then askin abart the row Ted and Charley 'ad 'ad. It weren't no row, it was like they always 'ad, just words, that was all, but them coppers made it into a row, then they said Charley 'ad killed Ted. I knows ee didn't, sir.' At this point, Jimmy burst into tears.

'Here, use this.' I passed him my handkerchief.

After a few more snuffles and a cup of tea Jimmy had calmed down. I found myself in somewhat of a dilemma. It would be foolish to explain to the lad that his boss was innocent and was only inside for the good of his health. The lad might talk, and those unknown assassins who, according to Holmes, were after Charley, would be forewarned. Holmes had to tackle this problem in his own inimitable way.

'Jimmy,' I said firmly, 'you must listen to me and do exactly what I say. Charley is now in prison where he will remain until the great detective, Sherlock Holmes, has solved the case.'

Jimmy's eyes, which only fifteen minutes before had been wet with tears, now sparkled with excitement. 'You are not to talk to anyone, Jimmy, not even your friend Mick. Do you understand?'

'Yes, sir.'

'Mrs Mayne is going away for a few days so keep well away from this house, and do not come near it again until Charley is free. Now listen carefully, I have a special mission for you.'
Jimmy sat bolt upright, agog to hear what he must do.
'I want you to be at 221B Baker Street at 8 o' clock sharp when Mr Holmes will see you.'

His mouth fell open. 'Mr Sherlock Holmes,' he whispered.

'Make sure you keep out of sight of anyone who knows you work for Charley, and do not go home. Here is a shilling, use it wisely.'

'Thank you, sir, thank you, sir.'

Jimmy's euphoria was wonderful to behold. Two magic words had transformed his life. The young sweep, whose tear-stained face was now serious as he contemplated the mission he had been given, left by the back door.

After Mrs Mayne had been safely delivered to her mother's home in Battersea I made my way to Baker Street where Holmes was waiting. Impatient as ususal.

'You took your time, Watson. What kept you?'

By the time I had finished my lengthy explanation Holmes was somewhat mollified, but to my dismay he was still intent on solving this case in three days. It was then that Holmes revealed that he had earlier experienced little difficulty in confirming the identity of, and discovering more about, the owner of the heraldic crest displayed on the side of the carriage belonging to the beautiful, mysterious woman whom Holmes and I had previously encountered in the street, and from whose home, Altair House, Charley had confessed to purloining two precious rubies. Lady Loubes-Bernac.

It was common knowledge that since Lady Loubes-Bernac's husband had died, she saw no one except family and her Indian friends. Gaining admittance to her home, Altair

House, was an impossibility even for Holmes. Her late husband, Brigadier Loubes-Bernac, had received the accolade of a knighthood for his devoted service in India. Only once during my short service in India had our paths crossed. He had been staying with my commanding officer for a few days during Empire Day celebrations and had complained about chest pains. My C.O. imagined the worst, thinking it could only be a heart condition caused by the strenuous exertions and nervous tension all officers had suffered throughout the Second Afghan War. He sent for me immediately and I was able to put his mind at rest. The pains were not incurred by the Brigadier's wartime exploits, nor was the patient amused when I diagnosed his complaint as poloitis.

'What does that mean, Doctor?' he had growled.

'An excess of polo during the past two days, sir.'

In India her ladyship had enjoyed an enviable reputation for her breadth of knowledge on Indian history and for the many monographs she had written on Indian temples and holy places. I seem to remember, from idle chatter in the mess, that the Loubes-Bernacs were always hard-up, three boys at Eton having drained their resources. All these facts I imparted to Holmes, whose eyes gleamed when I mentioned their financial straits. After contemplating the ceiling for some minutes, he weighed up the present situation.

'Despite what you have told me, Watson, the lady is not now short of a penny or two. She lives in a large luxurious house in the most expensive area of London, she owns a mansion on the Isle of Wight only a stone's throw from Osborne House, and has a large retinue of servants in both establishments. There is no doubt in my mind that with her Indian connections Lady Loubes-Bernac must, on occasions, visit the queen when she's at home in her island retreat. But, Watson, where does she obtain the means to maintain her life style?'

Holmes, who never ceases to amaze me, suddenly sat on the floor, his legs crossed, his back erect, looking for all the world like a smiling *Buddha*. He crossed his arms over his chest and carried on with the conversation as if this was his normal posture.

'Tomorrow, my friend, we will, all three of us, investigate different threads of this fascinating case which had its origins in India over thirty years ago.'

'Three of us, Holmes?'

'Yes. Your vigil will be to keep a morning watch on her ladyship's house in Belgrave Square and note all the comings and goings. Jimmy must get down to the docks, and I shall arise early like the proverbial bird and catch my worm, in the form of a train bound for Portsmouth, where I shall board a ferry for the Isle of Wight.'

Holmes had said of all cases this was my case, but I failed to see any connection between Thuggeeism, events in India and the death of a chimney sweep in his own back yard. While Holmes strummed a plaintive air on his violin, I sat wracking my brains. The clues to the case were not only thin on the ground, they were literally on the ground. A corpse, a cord tightly tied round the victim's neck, a pick axe, a bag, a strange smell of burnt sugar, and two precious rubies.

After we had finished dinner and were enjoying coffee accompanied by some very fine old port, Mrs Hudson entered, with a face as long as my friend's fiddle, to announce the arrival of a person, a mere boy, more beggarly and begrimed than any she had yet seen.

'Show him up, Mrs Hudson, the more beggarly, the more useful.'

Jimmy crept into the room like a stage struck schoolgirl waiting to see a great actor. He stood immobile, gazing at his hero, and at last managed to whisper the magic words. 'Mr Holmes.'

'Yes, Jimmy, I am he. Now you sit down,' said Holmes pulling out a chair for the lad,' and tell me exactly what you told Inspector Lestrade, and more to the point, what you failed to tell him.'

The boy took a deep breath. 'All they was interested in, sir, was the row, and they kept saying as 'ow Charley 'ad threatened to kill Ted, but he never. They was always shouting at each other, it didn't mean nuffin, and sometimes they took a swing at each other, but it was sort of fun with 'em, and we used to cheer 'em on. The Inspector 'ad me saying that they'd come to blows, but they 'adn't this time.'

'Why was that, Jimmy?'

'Some 'ow I think it was a bit more serious.'

33

'Ah!' said Holmes, placing his hands together, 'do I take it that you failed to mention the real cause of their argument to the police?'

'Yes, sir.'

'Very well, but now, Jimmy, you must divulge what you know, you must come clean.'

'I saw Charley slip summat to Ted, I wasn't supposed to see, but it looked like a jewel, like the jewels the Queen 'as in her crown. Ted looked at it for a moment and then asked him 'ow many there were. "Lots," said Charley.

'Well why didn't you bring the whole bloomin box,' shouted Ted. Then they noticed me and Mick watching, so they sent us 'ome.'

'Good work, my lad. Now you listen carefully, and by carrying out my precise instructions, you may be able to help Charley.'

'You mean they will let 'im come out of the can?'

'It is possible.'

The boy sat on a stool and gazed like a spaniel into his master's face.

'On no account, as Dr Watson has already mentioned, must you return home. You will, I am sure, have some relations not too far away.'

'My gran lives in the next street, sir.'

'Very well, go straight to your grandmother when you leave here, and stay the night. First thing tomorrow morning I want you to go down to the docks. Ask around, find out whether there are vacancies for cabin boys but,' said Holmes as he leant forward, 'you are only interested in ships that ply their trade between London and Indian ports. When you have the answer you must return here, and I will reward you with a shilling for your labours.'

'The other gentleman 'as already given me a shilling, sir.'

'You are, indeed, an honest lad, Jimmy, and tomorrow when you return Dr Watson will reward you with another shilling.'
'Thank you sir,' gulped Jimmy.

Looking back over my notes on this case I see that Holmes left Baker Street, at 5.15 the following morning, to catch the Portsmouth Express. The train conveniently connected with the ferry, which meant he stepped on to terra firma at Fishbourne no later than 10 o'clock. It was only when he returned to Baker Street that I learned of his *modus operandi*.

He called at the tradesman's entrance to the Loubes-Bernac mansion disguised as a gipsy, endowed with the gift of seeing not only into the future but able, if the atmosphere was conducive, to read the past. Her Ladyship was away, so too was the butler, and with great good fortune the cook, chambermaid, and kitchen maid were eager to have their fortunes told.

Gazing into a crystal ball, he foretold of a marriage for the chamber maid, who was a pretty slip of a girl, a death in the family for the cook, who would stand to inherit a modicum, and a change of situation for the kitchen maid, who had already let it be known that she was fed up with washing-up at all hours of the day and night. When it came to describing the past, he felt a distinct change in the atmosphere. 'As the mists clear,' he had said, 'I see movement at night, a gate opening, a carriage driving in, doors ajar, and dark figures gliding along corridors.'

'That is exactly what they do,' said the kitchen maid excitedly. 'They scare me with their .... '

'Hush' said the cook sharply.

'They do scare me something rotten. Their white heads float along the corridor like ghosts. They frighten me, I want to get away from this place.'

'They frighten me too,' said the chamber maid, 'and when they go they never leave me anything, not like proper visitors, and why do they always arrive at night?'

They had all crossed my friend's hand with a silver three-penny piece, but Holmes had not the heart to deprive them of their hard earned cash. Before leaving he pressed into the right hand of each woman a three-penny piece, saying it would bring them luck.

While Holmes was continuing his investigation in the Isle of Wight I was keeping a vigil outside Her Ladyship's house in Belgrave Square. My notes at this point are a little sketchy but I remember being gratified to find the gardens in the centre of the square open, and a bench conveniently placed, from where I could observe the comings and goings, and at the same time sit in comfort. It was a windless sunny day, the sort of weather that enabled me to forget my rheumatism, enjoy watching the gardeners at work, the constant stream of hansoms round the square, and for once, read *The Times* thoroughly. During the whole morning only five people called at *Altair House.* Surprisingly the first three callers were Sikhs, immaculately dressed in white, their turbans ornamented with jewels that glittered in the early morning sun. The front door opened as if of its own accord, because no hand or figure was visible. The fourth caller was a gentleman of the cloth. A person, whom I took to be the butler, opened the door and spoke for a few seconds before closing it again, leaving the poor man gazing at a magnificent leonine brass knocker. Shortly afterwards the door opened again, to reveal the remote, mysterious but beautiful, lady of the carriage. When I remonstrated with Holmes, refusing to believe that someone so beautiful, whose smile reached her eyes, whose whole being was angelic, could be in anyway connected with the murder of Ted Miller, he snorted derisively.

'Your hypothesis, my dear Watson, is untenable.'

The lady in question stood talking for a few moments to the clergyman, whose countenance, as he retraced his steps across the square, was one of puzzlement. The fifth caller was a small, bespectacled man, carrying an attaché case. He gave two short raps, easily audible from where I sat, and almost immediately the door opened and he literally slid inside.

Holmes could hardly contain himself when I expounded on my morning vigil. I have rarely seen him so excited, so enthused over what seemed to be a report of little significance. All the worry about the Baskerville case had melted away. Jimmy too, was able to bathe in the aura of Holmes' approbation. His report on the day's activities in dockland was exactly what my friend had expected to hear. There were two ships lying in the Pool of London registered in Bombay. The lad was bright. He had even discovered that both ships had followed the same route from Bombay to Aden, through the Red Sea, and the Suez Canal, thence to London, stopping at Gibraltar and Vigo.

'The route is of no import, but the time of arrival and departure is paramount to my investigation,' murmured Holmes, who could hardly wait for Jimmy to finish. *The Star of India*, we learnt, was flying the *Blue Peter* and about to sail after four days in port. *The Ranee* was expected to be in port for another two nights, and leave on the morning tide of the third day.

'Excellent, Jimmy, quite excellent,' smiled Holmes. 'Now you must return to your grandmother, and stay put until you hear news of Charley's release.'

After Jimmy had departed I picked up *The Times*, which neither of us had read, only to discover several letters that had arrived by the first post.

'Interesting,' said Holmes, as he perused one of the missives. 'This is from Exeter, but why do I not recognise the calligraphy?' He stood for some moments before handing it to me. 'Watson, this is from Mortimer, Henry Baskerville's doctor. He has a problem he cannot solve, but it may well fall within your province.'

'I very much doubt it, Holmes. According to this letter Baskerville is fading away, eats very little, sleeps with his door locked and swears that in the small hours he hears the hound baying. It is all in the mind and my middle name is neither Freud nor Adler.'

'Nonetheless, Watson I am sure that in your company he would recover his equilibrium. I would really like you to make tracks and leave for Devon on the night train.'

'No, Holmes. For once I am going to dig my heels in, but I promise you that as soon as you have solved the murder of the chimney sweep, I will be on my way.'

Holmes laughed. You want to be at the kill do you?'

'I certainly do.'

'Well, Watson, it may come to that. Our next step,' he said, 'is to have a word with Lestrade, who should be here at any moment in answer to a wire I sent before leaving Fishbourne.'
The words had scarce been uttered before we heard the bell ring and Lestrade's heavy footsteps ascending the stairs. Holmes opened the door.

'Enter, Inspector, your timing is perfect. Now your case has been solved to my satisfaction we can get down to business.'

'Solved!' expostulated Lestrade. 'You never cease to amaze me, Holmes. Who would want to murder a chimney sweep, and more to the point, why?'

'I will be able to reveal everything tomorrow, when I have secured the evidence I need to incriminate the assassins and convince a jury of their guilt and Charley's innocence. Lestrade, your case will be solved to your satisfaction at 3 o'clock tomorrow afternoon.'

The Inspector sat up. I could see him thinking that here was another case solved, with all the publicity and kudos requisite for his promotional prospects.

Lestrade found it difficult to understand the workings of Holmes' brilliant mind, the mental capacity of a man who employed such monumental powers of deduction.

'In what way can the force assist you, Holmes?'

'It is essential that tomorrow you take a posse of your best men to guard the front and back exits to *Altair House* in Belgrave Square. Be in position by 3 o'clock on the dot. Do not delay, Lestrade, for it will be a matter of life and death.'

Lestrade left, not quite singing to himself, but with a rare smile on his ruddy countenance.

For years I had become accustomed to Holmes' assumption that I would be there and waiting to do whatever had to be done, but for once I was becoming extremely peeved at being kept in the dark.

'Holmes, is it not time you told me what is happening tomorrow, and why you need such a large police presence, and if you need so much assistance, why is it that you have not yet called upon my services. Instead you suggested I made tracks for Baskerville Hall.'

'Sorry, my dear fellow,' and to give my friend his due, he was truly abject, 'I assumed you would follow my reasoning, especially after your careful observation of those visitors to *Altair House* from our dominions overseas. Of course I need you, no one is more necessary to my well being than my closest friend. At 3 o'clock tomorrow, and not a moment sooner, I want you to stand outside the drawing room window of Her Ladyship's house. Be armed, and on your guard, dear friend, because it could be a bloody business. Be prepared for fireworks, we are dealing with ruthless, desperate characters.'

'Where will you be, Holmes?'

'Inside the room, Watson.'

'Then I shall come with you. Surely it is safer for both of us to apprehend these felons?'

Holmes shook his head.

41

'We would never gain admittance, Watson. You, yourself, told me how a well-meaning clergyman, doing his parish rounds, was treated. Turned away, you said. Believe me, Watson, when I say that this is the only way to obtain the evidence we need to prove Charley's innocence.'

It was never any good arguing with Holmes once his mind was made up, but if he spoke of a peril then I knew the situation would be fraught with danger. Sleep was a fitful bedfellow, and in the early hours of the morning I rose, cleaned and oiled my revolver and sat on my bed, imagining the worst. Holmes, my dearest friend, will this be the end? Have you gone beyond the bounds and tempted fate once too often? It was the most wretched night of my life.

I kept an eye on *Altair House* well before the appointed time, though I had the good sense to remain hidden behind a large plane tree. By 2.45 Lestrade and his men were ready and assembled in West Halkin Street. Five minutes later Lady Loubes-Bernac received a visitor, another Sikh, a tall man, again immaculately robed, with his turban ornamented with three large rubies.

It is from my notes, that were so quickly scrawled, that I am able to relate exactly what happened in the drawing room of *Altair House* on that eventful afternoon. The visitor was admitted to the house, and shown into the drawing room, where he waited for Lady Loubes-Bernac to appear, not sitting as one would expect, but prowling round the room, examining the fireplace, and the family pictures, and in particular the large wooden shield depicting the family crest.

A few minutes later the lady entered, followed by two more Sikhs, who strangely enough were not wearing their turbans. The visitor bowed to his fellow countrymen, and then to the lady of the house, who held out her hands towards his face. He surprised her by taking both hands in his and lowering them to her sides. She took a step back, whereupon the tall visitor knelt before her. She laughed merrily at the gesture and stood directly in front of him, her feet touching his knees. Again she lifted both hands, but this time she could reach his turban. Carefully she loosened elaborately fashioned claws, that held the three rubies in place until she was able to hold them in her hands. One of her minions kept his back to the door, while the other deftly opened a wall cupboard whose small door was shaped like a wooden shield. From the cupboard he withdrew a leather bag, and a small cashbox, still with the key in it, which he opened.

Lady Loubes-Bernac took a closer look at the jewels in her hand before slipping them into the leather bag. For a second she stood transfixed, before giving a blood-curdling scream, a scream that was clearly audible in the street, but my instructions had been explicit, 3 o'clock at the window and not a moment before, Holmes had said. It took all my self-control to wait another four minutes and not rush my fences.
'These are fakes,' she screamed, 'these are glass.'

The kneeling man leapt to his feet as the angry woman threw the rubies across the room. At the same time one attendant ripped a family picture off the wall and tore the cord off the frame, while the other one hurled himself at the newcomer. The lady kept on yelling, 'Kill him! Kill him! Kill

43

him!' but the visitor was not to be taken so easily. He seized two swords from Charley's pattern of swords, and using one as a sabre and the other as a rapier, bravely defended himself, but despite Holmes prowess with the sword, for it was Holmes disguised as a Sikh, as I am sure you have guessed, he was no match for the raging woman and her two bodyguards. She too snatched up a sword, and while Holmes was concentrating on keeping the woman and one of the men at bay, the other leapt from a table and with one movement, managed to pull the picture cord tightly round his neck, dragging my friend into a prone position on the floor, knocking his turban off in the process.

At 3 o'clock precisely Lestrade, who had heard the commotion, burst through the front door, and into the drawing room, while I took up my position outside the house. The man with the noose still in his hand took a running jump straight through the window, splaying the glass in every direction. He was up and running but there were too many pedestrians around for me to take a shot at him. My only thought was for my friend, who might be mortally wounded. Regardless of the jagged glass I jumped through the window and rushed to Holmes, who was lying winded on the floor, struggling for breath, with the marks of the cord still painfully prominent round his neck.

'Watson,' he said, 'Watson, my friend, a few seconds more and all would have been over, but it had to be this way.'

Lestrade arrested Lady Loubes-Bernac and one of her minions. The window was boarded up, the drawing room locked and a police presence left in the house. Later, and this was a first, he joined us for dinner at *Goldini's,* renowned for its Italian cuisine. Lestrade, who was unusually generous in his praise for my friend's brilliance in solving a bizarre crime, was impatient to hear how the evidence had been obtained. If Lestrade's credence in court was to stand up to a counsel's penetrating questions he needed to have all the facts of the case at his finger tips. He quizzed Holmes, who was rather quiet, in fact he looked quite depressed, not his usual ebullient self after solving a crime.

'Come on, Holmes,' said Lestrade, 'how did you guess Lady Loubes-Bernac was instrumental in having Ted Miller murdered?'

'It was no guess, Lestrade, it was simple deduction. The reason for Ted Miller's death lay in *Altair House,* for he and Charley had swept the chimneys on that fatal day. I knew of the lady's interest in Asia, and I recognised the Thuggee rites, and realised that Charley Mayne and the two young boys could be the next victims.

Mick, sensibly, kept well away from Charley's place but Jimmy called to see Mrs Mayne, which is why I insisted he made himself scarce and stayed with a relative. You, Lestrade, were the only means of protecting Charley, which is why I persuaded him to give himself up. Charley was the catalyst. It was he who discovered, on a ledge in the drawing room chimney, a metal box with the key still in the lock. It contained rubies.

There was only one reason why it was in such a strange position. Any port in a storm, was the answer. Certain transactions often took place in the drawing room and the lady who conducted them was suddenly disturbed by two sharp raps on the front door. Her visitor was earlier than expected. One of her minions, whom I will call a Thug, was standing by the fireplace with the box in his hand, and for him the easiest, most convenient hiding place was in the chimney. The lady closed the wall cupboard, its door shaped like a shield, before the visitor, a jeweller from Bond Street, famed for his settings of exotic jewellery, was shown into the room. His visits always coincided with the arrival of *The Ranee*, in the Port of London, although he was unaware of the fact. The ship, registered in Bombay, carried an interesting crew who all practised Thuggeeism.'

I gasped, 'You were right, Holmes, then the sect is still extant and practising.'

'It is, although the members visit *Altair House* in the guise of Sikhs I doubt whether they have descended, like all good Sikhs, from the dissenters of Brahmanical Hinduism. The turban was a passport providing a simple means of carrying their booty for all to see, and yet paradoxically, not be seen.

The jeweller, who never asked pertinent questions, was not told how the jewels entered the country, but more of that in a moment. There was complete trust between the protagonists in this drama, the lady and the fence. As soon as the rubies arrived at *Altair House,* so too did the jeweller. He collected the stones in a small suede bag, which was returned the following day with the proceeds, once he had had time to examine the rubies.'

I opened my mouth, but Holmes forestalled me.

'You are about to ask about the source of the precious stones, but think, Watson, think about the lady's talents.'

'Of course, Holmes, of course. I have been exceedingly slow. It may all stem from her deep knowledge of holy places scattered throughout India.'

'Precisely, my dear fellow. The Thugs, dressed as Sikhs, visited shrine after shrine abstracting genuine stones and replaced them with the glass beads that ornamented their turbans. The process was reversed when they reached England and called on Lady Loubes-Bernac. In her old cash box she kept dozens of imitation stones which she would change for the genuine priceless jewels of India.'

Lestrade, sat enthralled. 'Amazing, Holmes! The wit of the first class criminal can never be underestimated.'

'This lady is certainly a criminal, almost par excellence,' said Holmes with a wry smile. 'She has carried out a successful operation for over thirty years. Fifteen of those years in this country. If *The Ranee* docked at Portsmouth the stones were delivered to her mansion on the Isle of Wight. You could say,' he said suddenly with a burst of schoolboy humour, 'that no stone has been left unturned. It all started, of course, when her three sons were at Eton. Remember those idle chats in the mess, Watson, about the penurious state of the Loubes-Bernacs? But, fortunately, my friend, even the most experienced criminal slips up.

The lady never imagined for one moment that a noose fashioned from Indian hemp, a bag used to carry kindling, a pickaxe, and a smell of burnt sugar would lead directly to the solving of the death of an unfortunate sweep. She was also foolish enough, this lady with the angelic smile, to visit the scene of crime.' He looked at me with a sardonic smile, 'There is one thing you must remember, Watson, all that glisters is not gold.'

At that point we were interrupted by the headwaiter who mentioned, sotto voce, to Lestrade that there was a policeman in reception wanting to speak to him urgently. Holmes smiled to himself. I have no doubt that he was thinking another case might come his way. I too hoped so, for it would keep him from harking back to a failure not of his making.

When Lestrade returned he stood for a moment staring at Holmes, as though he wanted to share something with him, then with a hardly perceptible shake of his head, made his apologies promising before he left to give orders for the ships in dock to be searched. He would leave no stone unturned in the hunt for the thug who had attempted to garrotte my friend.

After the inspector's departure Holmes sat tapping the table with his coffee spoon.

'What was he saying, Watson? Something of great importance, I have no doubt.'

'Intuition, Holmes. Not like you, my friend, to make so much of so little. Lestrade has probably been called to a crime that, on second thoughts, he felt that he could solve without your expertise.

'Rubbish, Watson. The pain in his eyes, the clenched jaw, a man wanting to speak out but dare not. Deduction, Watson, not intuition.'

I could get nothing more out of him, highly unusual after a case has culminated so successfully. It was quite late when I called a cab; first of all Baker Street then home back home to Paddington, where Mary would still be up waiting for me as she always did. Only when the cab stopped at 221B did Holmes raise his voice to declare that the murder of the chimney sweep had not been solved to his satisfaction. Of the five hundred cases he had solved over the past few years as a consulting detective, two gave him no pleasure. Yet another murderer had escaped. Stapleton, and now someone dressed as a Sikh. Something he had hoped would never happen again.

CHAPTER FOUR

The morning after Holmes had solved that spine-chilling murder was a morning I would like to forget, but when writing memoirs, verisimilitude is everything. My friend was reading *The Times* when suddenly he leapt to his feet. 'Oh my God!' he cried out, 'this explains everything. I should have known something was wrong. Not like my brother to miss a concert.'

At that moment I thought that Mycroft must have had a serious heart attack, which would explain why he had not put in an appearance at St James's Hall for a concert on the previous Wednesday, but that was not the case. Holmes thrust the paper into my hands and pointed to a small paragraph on page two.

It said very little, and only by reading between the lines did we realise that a few sentences reporting the arrest of a man on special duties at the Home Office, was none other than Mycroft, Holmes's elder brother. *The unnamed man, well-known in London clubs, has committed a crime against the state and is being held in the Tower at the Queen's pleasure.*

The article went on to say that the man had been caught spying, late at night, and as papers relating to matters of state were missing, the man would be charged with treason.

Holmes was devastated. 'Watson, a crime against the state is high treason, and hanging is the only way such cases are dealt with. It is obvious now why Lestrade was called away. This is the matter that he desperately wanted to impart, but had he opened his mouth I have no doubt it would have cost him his job.'

My friend said there was nothing for it. He would, first of all, call at the Home Office before making his way to The Tower. Not alone, I told him. He made no objection, just a slight nod of the head. I had never in all the years we had known each other seen him so tense. Before we left he downed an usually large measure of cocaine. In my view, that was no substitute for his misery.

The cab travelled swiftly down Oxford Street and into Regent Street but by the time we reached Waterloo Place it was impossible to make further progress. There were thousands of men and women converging on Trafalgar Square, all screaming and shouting *down with the monarchy.* Many were armed with knives or sticks, even pokers and iron bars. Some were waving red flags.

'Anarchists' shouted the cab driver. 'Just like Bloody Sunday all over again. There is no way I can go any further, sir. Look, sirs,' he said, pointing towards Pall Mall, 'the Grenadier Guards are trying to close it off. Hundreds of 'em, but they won't be any more successful than they were on Bloody Sunday two years ago, and I bet that writer Shaw don't put in an appearance this time. No one would ever be able to 'ear 'im.'

'Why do they behave like this?' yelled Holmes whose temper was sorely stretched.

'Holmes,' and I had to shout above the noise, 'you know why. Poverty, starvation and thirty percent of the population without jobs. Displaced families, men women and children sleeping in the streets. The working-class can only make their views known by rioting and violence.'

'Yes,' he said suddenly calming down, 'a sad time, Watson. Six attempts on the life of our queen already. Who knows how many more? If only Lord Salisbury would give our beloved queen advice and comfort when she is at her lowest ebb. Even advise her not to salt away untold riches, but to share them.'

This did not sound like the Holmes I knew. He was suffering from shock engendered by Mycroft's imprisonment and the possible outcome.

'Watson, is the monarchy so unpopular that it will come to an end with the death of Victoria?'

'I doubt it, my friend. It is an institution that will go on for ever.'

The cabbie was getting impatient. 'What do you want me to do?' he yelled.

'Turn around,' shouted Holmes,' and make for The Tower.'

After driving through a city of discontent we reached our destination. Holmes had made up his mind to call on the Constable and demand access to Mycroft. Unfortunately that was not possible because the Constable, on Her Majesty's orders, had been called to Holyrood House in Edinburgh.

The Deputy Governor, whom I had met in India, was sympathetic, but had been given orders not to discuss the case nor allow anyone access to Mycroft. Holmes was so enraged by this approach that he decided, despite his earlier thoughts on the matter, that he would risk contacting Lestrade in such a way that the inspector would not be compromised.

On our journey back to Baker Street Holmes asked me to drop in at the Diogenes Club. I knew that persuading members to talk would be like getting blood out of a stone, but the waiters might be more forthcoming. The club, situated in Pall Mall, to which Mycroft belonged, was unlike any other.

There are many misanthropes in the city who have no need for the company of others, yet they are not ill-disposed to comfortable chairs and the latest periodicals. Mycroft was a founder member of the Diogenes, a club facing his lodgings, which embraced the most unsociable and unclubbable men in town. All of whom preferred not to communicate with each other. Only in the Stranger's Room was talking allowed. I readily agreed to visit the club later that day. Needless to say I was curious to take a look at these unsociable fellows, but late in the evening, I thought, after they had enjoyed a good meal and a few stiff whiskies, always guaranteed to loosen the tongue.

As soon as we entered the house Mrs Hudson thrust a letter into the hands of my friend. The messenger, she said, who delivered the missive, did not wait for a reply. Holmes, recognising Lestrade's hand, opened it there and then.

'Watson,' he said in strangled tones, 'Lestrade has to be telepathic.'

Telepathy! A medium Holmes had never acknowledged. The inspector had scribbled a few lines, stating that every policeman in London had been placed on twenty-four hour duty. The chaos gave him the opportunity to slip away just before midnight and not be missed. He would wait for us under the cover of trees surrounding the Serpentine in Hyde Park.

It was nine in the evening when I walked into the Diogenes Club. The porter never queried whether I was a member, thus giving me the opportunity to order a brandy, and sit down in the main clubroom whilst observing two members playing chess. Not a word was uttered. One sharp rap for check and two raps for checkmate. A few who had eaten and drunk too well were half asleep, one was snoring in the most bestial manner, but no one uttered a word. A waiter entered and gave the disturber of the peace a jolt and all was silence once again. I then shifted to the Stranger's Room and listened to the gossip. To begin with, the main topic of conversation covered racing at Ascot during the afternoon, their gains, but mostly their losses. Only when two fellows entered discussing Mycroft, did the room come alive.

Mycroft, it seems, was not the same man to any two people. Some saw him as a dedicated Whitehall highflyer, loyal to

Queen and country, completely focussed on doing what he had to do. Others thought him introverted and reserved. They were the ones who believed he held too much power in Whitehall. Two members discussed at length whether, throughout the years, he could have been a spy in the employ of a foreign power, and his arrest might be justified. They favoured France or Germany. Others profoundly disagreed with the idea that someone like Mycroft, who was a confirmed royalist, would ever become involved in anything so heinous. Another older man, sitting in the far corner of the room, said Mycroft Holmes would not be incarcerated for too long because his clever brother would get him off the hook. 'Not this time,' said a red-headed fellow, who had been staring at me for some minutes. He suddenly crossed the room and stood in front of me.

'The clever detective,' he told the members, 'will soon know everything that has been uttered in this room. This man here is Dr Watson. He is not a member here, therefore let us call him a spy.'

I apologised and left hurriedly, not having learnt anything to help Holmes in his search for the truth.

We arrived at the Serpentine to find Lestrade waiting for us, well hidden in the bushes. There was a full moon but fortunately scudding clouds blotted out the light from time to time, providing a little more cover. I stood on guard, my pistol at the ready in order to create a diversion should anyone get too close. Lestrade, it seems, was only too ready to talk. He told us he had fully expected to be given the task of arresting the unnamed man at the centre of the Home

Office enquiry but he was sidestepped. The reason became transparently clear when his chief inspector told him that he knew the man's brother and had worked with him on many cases. Therefore, as he told Holmes, there was no doubt in his mind about the identity of the unnamed man.

Lestrade was furious. 'Not the first time,' he fumed, 'to be taken off a case. It was the same with the Ripper murders. My boss James Munro unexpectedly resigned and Inspector Frederick Abberline took over. After that the whole matter was kept under wraps and the public in the dark.' Lestrade was almost spitting when he said, 'All Abberline had to say about the Ripper Case was that there were five hundred inquests into unexplained deaths in the Whitechapel District in 1888, so why make such a fuss about five women who were probably prostitutes? History, Holmes, has repeated itself. This time the case concerning your brother Mycroft, a case that should have been mine, has been handed to Inspector Jemmet.'

Holmes waited for the inspector's wrath to subside before telling him that he had been to The Tower and was refused access to Mycroft. Lestrade, peering round to make sure no one was in earshot, told him that visiting The Tower was a wasted exercise. Mycroft had already been moved to Dartmoor, where no visitors were allowed. There, he said, the prisoner would wait until the case came up for trial. Lestrade, having eavesdropped on several conversations at the Yard, told us that Mycroft would probably be charged with treason.

'But why?' asked Holmes. 'Crime against the state is high treason. Without doubt it means the death penalty, so why treason?'

'Because, Mr Holmes, it is possible that if it were high treason too much would be revealed, whereas, as things stand, he can be kept for months, even years, in that hideous prison on Dartmoor without the case being heard. I have heard whispers that it is all to do with the monarchy. Yet from another source I hear that another power is involved but I cannot see that myself.'

'Holmes,' I whispered urgently, 'there are two men approaching from the north side.'

'Holmes shook Lestrade's hand. 'I am greatly indebted to you, but I will not contact you again. Too dangerous for you to be seen with me until I have solved this case.'

'That, I am afraid, Mr Holmes, you will never be able to do. Nevertheless, good luck.'

'Watson, fire a shot. It will disturb all the lovers and drunks and give the intruders something to think about. Meanwhile Lestrade can make tracks towards the Albert Hall and we will go north.'

As we walked back to Baker Street Holmes stopped suddenly. 'Watson,' he whispered, 'you know I have said many times that I would be lost without my Boswell. There are several cases you have chronicled, but never publicised which remain safely locked away in your old tin despatch box at Cox and Company's Bank. You know what I am trying to say, my friend?'

'I am not obtuse, Holmes. I shall, of course make sure that the notes on Mycroft's case are absolutely confidential, but I have a strong feeling that you may eventually change your mind. Let us call it intuition.'

Holmes smiled a weary smile, then shook his head.

CHAPTER FIVE

Mrs Hudson was quite perturbed to be knocked up in the early hours of the morning. 'Mr Holmes, Mr Holmes, are you all right, sir?'

'Yes, Mrs Hudson.'

'I must say you look quite drawn.'

'The light, Mrs Hudson, the light. Say no more. All I ask is that you re-set your alarm. Doctor Watson will be staying the night because we have to catch the 7.30 train to Exeter which means we will need to breakfast at 6 o'clock, no later.'

The good lady, who was used to my friend's sudden decisions merely smiled, saying, 'Yes, sir. Of course, sir.'

'Goodnight Mrs Hudson or rather good morning.' he said, heading for the sitting room. Mrs H closed her door, still looking bemused.

'Holmes,' I said, following him into the room, 'presumably you intend to visit Sir Henry and maybe stay at Baskerville Hall?'

'Indeed. In his state of health he will be only too pleased to have our protection. It will also give you a chance to discuss his condition with Dr Mortimer.'

'His condition, Holmes, as you and I know full well, will be the same in a week's time. You have only one thought in your mind. Clearing Mycroft's name. Proving his innocence eclipses the desire to trace Stapleton, whose bestial hound was instrumental in the deaths of Sir Charles Baskerville and a wretched convict on Grimpen Moor.'

'It is not just Mycroft's name I need to clear, Watson. My name too will be besmirched. A consulting detective, par excellence, will be out of favour with the gentry, with foreign clients, and most of all, with Scotland Yard.'

'You surely do not believe that the outcome of Mycroft's case will affect you in the smallest measure?'

'This could be a diabolical plot, Watson, obliquely aimed at someone close to Mycroft.'

'Are you saying that whatever the outcome it will affect you?'

'Yes, Watson, that is exactly what I am saying. Now you need to be horizontal. Get some sleep, my dear fellow,' he said, picking up his Stradivarius.

My friend's way of coping with stress was to stroke the strings of the gem for which he had paid fifty-five shillings in Tottenham Court Road. The instrument, worth over five hundred guineas, was always kept in its case, well away from all the chemical equipment and burners. It was more than a toy to Holmes. It was a treasure. My friend said that I needed sleep. For once he was wrong.

For nearly an hour I listened to the strains of Mozart. Then I too began questioning what Mycroft was doing in his office at such a late hour. I knew, of course, that he audited the books in several government departments, and that for some time the accounts of all departments had been passed on to him. Mycroft's memory was prodigious. A great brain in which every detail was pigeonholed, which explained why many of his conclusions had become national policy. The powers that be were aware of his status, so why, then, did they allow him to be placed under arrest and incarcerated in The Tower without ever contacting his brother? Mulling over the various strands that were becoming embroiled in this case kept me awake. It was quite the worst case that Holmes had ever faced. There was no way he could begin his investigation until he had spoken with Mycroft. I knew he needed me with him, but for how long would we be in the West Country? It could be weeks before we had traced Stapleton. Mary would understand why I could not leave him at this juncture. An understanding and wonderful wife, who accepted these absences from time to time without a word of reproach.

On arrival at Baskerville Hall we were surprised to see a two-year-old boy attempting to fly a kite on the front lawn. He was shouting words a young child should never use because the kite had become entangled in a tree. Holmes immediately went to the child's aid. Despite his height he was not tall enough to reach the wind-blown toy, but with the aid of his stick, he dragged the kite down. The child, who was overjoyed, was then warned by my friend to note the direction of the wind and keep well clear of the trees if the wind was blowing in their direction.

At that point the front door opened and Mrs Stapleton emerged. She looked amazed, then flushed with pleasure as she came forward to shake hands.

'What a wonderful surprise, Mr Holmes. Sir Henry will be delighted to see you again.'

The child, who by now had heeded the advice he had been given, was playing out the string of the kite, and in perfect safety this time, his joy a delight to behold.

Holmes looked at Mrs Stapleton questioningly, then at the child. She was a different woman, a changed woman. Two years ago when we last met she was covered in bruises inflicted by her jealously brutal husband. The man who had escaped justice, the man who had given Holmes so many sleepless nights. Stapleton always referred to Beryl Stapleton as his sister, never his wife. It was only when Sir Henry fell in love with her that he all but killed her in his rage.

Beryl Stapleton knew exactly what Holmes was thinking. She told us that when Stapleton vanished she was six months pregnant. Sir Henry generously allowed her to continue living at Merripit House until Arthur was born. After that she became his housekeeper, but as we learnt later, never his mistress. Sir Henry's moral propensities would never allow the woman he loved to be smeared by innuendo. He observed the proprieties. There was no question of marriage, not while there was any possibility that her husband was still alive.

At dinner that evening Sir Henry, who had been initially tight-lipped and visibly strained, relaxed noticeably over an excellent decanter of claret, but emphatically declared that he continued to hear the baying of a hound in the small hours. Holmes promised that we would not leave until the matter had been resolved and that I would be constantly by his side. Needless to say, I knew, although Holmes was loath to admit it, that his visit to Baskerville Hall was a sprat to catch a mackerel. In fact, two mackerels. His prime motivation was to gain access to Mycroft and secondly, to continue his search for Stapleton.

Over coffee, much to my surprise, Holmes explained to Sir Henry that Stapleton was not the only reason that had brought him down to the West Country. On hearing of Mycroft's incarceration in The Tower, the baronet, who was appalled, immediately offered to be of help, if he could, in solving the enigma of Mycroft's arrest. He was quite taken aback when he learnt that Mycroft, a government accountant and inter-departmental adviser, was now being held only fourteen miles away, having been transferred to the infamous Princeton prison, Dartmoor, on a charge of treason. Pondering for some time, he eventually came to the conclusion that the most damning evidence against Mycroft was that he had been apprehended in the building at night.

Holmes told him it was not surprising. His brother was unmarried. His work was his life. His lodgings were in Pall Mall. He walked round the corner into Whitehall every morning, returning every evening. If there were complications he would remain in his office until he had solved them. In fact, if the art of detection could be practised from an arm-chair, brother Mycroft would be the greatest criminal agent who had ever lived, but he had no energy and no ambition in that field of endeavour. My friend also told the baronet that there were many strands in this extraordinary affair, and for the moment all he needed was an introduction to the Governor of Dartmoor.

'Not that easy,' mused Sir Henry. 'My friend Sir John Falconby is a hard man, not a man to grant favours. The means to an end must be subtly played.' After cogitating for some time he smiled suddenly. 'Why not attend morning service at Tavistock Church on Sunday? The Reverend Pyke's sermons never last more than fifteen minutes.'

'Excellent' roared Holmes. 'An excellent suggestion, but first I think a visit to the church beforehand would not come amiss.'

After dinner, while taking the night air, I told Holmes that tracing Stapleton was a hopeless task and that he would do better to concentrate on Mycroft.

'Finding Stapleton, Watson, will be child's play. A bit like flying a kite, but one must first make sure which way the wind blows. As for the other matter, as I have stated before, I believe Mycroft's supposed crime is an ingenious plot to undermine my life as a consulting detective.'

As usual Holmes was talking in riddles. Flying a kite had little to do with the case, nor did I believe that anyone could possibly destroy his reputation as the most brilliant consulting detective in the kingdom, but I let the matter drop, knowing that all his intellectual skills would be concentrated on solving the wrongful arrest of his brother. Saving his own reputation would take second place.

Our bedrooms were adjacent, at the back of the house, overlooking a magnificent rose garden, with the moors providing a most spectacular backcloth. In London we always slept with our windows closed to keep out the stench, the noise and the fog but here in the countryside we left them wide open. The early morning birdsong, the quiet mooing of the cattle and the sweet smells of the countryside were pleasures to be enjoyed to the full. Shortly after one in the morning I was disturbed, thought at first that I was dreaming, but the baying of the hound was no dream. Holmes was also awake. 'Watson,' he shouted through the open window, 'can you hear me?'

'Yes, Holmes. I hear you and the extraneous sounds.' It was then that we heard Sir Henry cry out.

'Quickly, Watson, see what you can do for Sir Henry. I will investigate further afield.'

I ran to Sir Henry's room but the door was locked. At that moment, Beryl Stapleton appeared on the landing. 'He won't unlock the door, doctor. He never does.'

'He must,' I said grimly. After talking to him for some time I finally persuaded him to let me enter. He looked haggard, hardly the man who three hours before had entertained us at dinner. By the time he unlocked the door Mrs Stapleton had, wisely, returned to her room.

'So many sleepless nights, Doctor. I am sorry to have disturbed you. I fear it is all in my mind; the fear of this animal will remain with me for life. It will destroy me.'

I was able, in some measure, to reassure him when I explained that both Holmes and I had heard the animal.

'Yes, Sir Henry, we did' said Holmes on entering the room. ' I now know where the animal is being kept.'

'Congratulations, Holmes. We can then shoot the beast in the morning.'

'That is not a good idea,' replied Holmes. ' The animal must be left in captivity until the case has been solved.'

Sir Henry, like the gentleman he is, told Holmes that Mycroft was a more deserving case and that he must not waste time on domestic problems at Baskerville.

'By the time we leave, Sir Henry,' and Holmes was emphatic, 'I will have solved my brother's wrongful arrest and also apprehended Stapleton in this neck of the woods. This time he will not evade the law by escaping arrest.'

Sir Henry looked amazed. 'Is Beryl safe? Is young Arthur safe, with this vile man at large somewhere in this area?'

'He will never harm the child,' replied Holmes. 'Of that I am quite certain.'

As we left Sir Henry's room Mrs Stapleton emerged from the shadows. 'Did you give him anything, doctor, to calm him down?' she whispered.

'No, Mrs Stapleton, because I hope our words were a panacea.' As she thanked us we heard the key turn. Quickly I placed my fingers to her lips in case she made a sound. 'Early days, Mrs Stapleton, but I am sure the cure will eventually be effective.' It was impossible to see her eyes, but I knew she was unconvinced.

On returning to our rooms Holmes grimaced angrily. 'Watson, how could I have been so stupid? Come on into my room. We must rethink the return journey we took to Paddington two years ago after that wretched convict had been killed by Stapleton's hound.'

First he lit the oil-lamp, then his pipe. As we sat in the comfortable armchairs I wondered what on earth had happened on that tedious journey to rouse him in such a manner.

'Watson, think back. Why were we delayed some three or four hours on our return journey?'

'A murder, Holmes. The murder of an unidentified man.'

'Yes, my friend. A man whose clothes and luggage vanished. Now who would need a change of clothes, and luggage to make him look presentable when attempting to hire lodgings?'

'A beggar, perhaps?'

'Not a beggar, Watson.'

'Then it must be a fugitive escaping justice.'

'Yes, Watson, a fellow who had just committed murder.'

'Of course. Stapleton! It would help if we knew what sort of garments the victim had been wearing.'

Holmes agreed, but said we were too late. Stapleton would have wasted no time changing his clothes in order to create an acceptable persona before taking lodging in a nearby village, for he had to be close to Baskerville Hall. My friend was certain that Beryl Stapleton's husband was still in the area, but hoped sincerely that she would be unaware of the danger.

There was a chance that he might kidnap the child, an aspect that worried me, but Holmes was adamant in his belief that Stapleton would never risk kidnap when killing Sir Henry was his goal. The hound was a distraction and a decoy. Sir Henry, who was an excellent shot, was being goaded into going out on the moor and killing the beast. Fortunately Holmes nipped that idea in the bud. He was emphatic about the whereabouts of the hound. It would be kept in some old sheds on the Merripit Estate, where Stapleton once lived. The house was empty because no one had cared to rent it after the events of two years ago. The hound could be dealt with when Lestrade, with the aid of local police, surrounded the outbuildings. In the meantime the beast had to be fed and watered, a job Stapleton was hardly likely to hand to someone else. Complete secrecy could be his only cover, but we had to find his lodgings first before tracking him to the barn.

We decided that we would visit Tavistock immediately after breakfast the following day, to do some ferreting around. For Holmes, making contact with the Reverend Pyke was more important at that moment than laying hands on Stapleton.

CHAPTER SIX

After breakfast, for which Holmes had little appetite, Palmer, Sir Henry's groom, drove us into Tavistock, stopping outside the Lord Nelson, where we alighted. It was a cool, misty morning, excellent for nosing around a small market town, but Holmes decided that we would be too conspicuous. If Stapleton happened to be in the area he would recognise us immediately and take flight.

'He would recognise us, Holmes, but would we recognise him? He could have dyed his hair, grown a beard, even scarred his face in such a manner as to make recognition virtually impossible.'

'An easy man to spot, Watson, with the idiosyncratic movement of his right arm suggesting a fractured elbow many years ago and slightly hunched shoulders as he walks. Remember he is a naturalist, always peering down at bugs, beetles and other flora and fauna. Did he not discover the Vandaleur moth? Also let us not forget that the few words he uttered on the moor when we discovered that unfortunate convict, were not spoken in a Devonshire brogue, nor could you say that they were in standard English.'

Holmes, who had quite an ear for accents, said he had to be an Englishman who had lived abroad for some years, probably South Africa, suggested by the flat vowel sounds.

Within half an hour of arriving in Tavistock, Holmes took on the services of two local urchins as irregulars. Tom and Josh, aged ten and eleven, were overawed when they realised that the great Sherlock Holmes actually needed their help in a most important matter. Their eyes sparkled when they heard the great detective promise them each a shilling when they returned to St Leonard's graveyard with the information he desired. All they had to do was find out how many strangers were living in the area; strangers who could not have been around for more than two years.

When the lads had been despatched we made our way to St Leonard's Church, a twelfth century edifice in the centre of Tavistock. The west door was wide open but Holmes, who had little interest in church architecture, decided to wander round the graveyard. Inscriptions on tombstones never ceased to fascinate him.

'Watson,' he said, as he puffed away at his pipe, 'why is it that I have never yet read an offensive dedication to any of the deceased who lie interred in graves all over the world? Why such honeyed words when the truth would be more believable?'

'Holmes, you must agree that the greater the person, the greater the plaudits. If you want the truth, then read historical biography or, in the present time, look at the work of reputable journalists, especially in *The Manchester Guardian* and *The Daily Telegraph and Morning Post*.'

'Yes, yes, Watson, you are right.'

It was then we saw the vicar approaching, accompanied by two women who were laughing. The older woman was clutching the younger woman's arm for support.

'Mother and daughter,' said Holmes. 'They have come to discuss the marriage ritual.'

'Or burial, Holmes.'

'No, no, my dear fellow. They look far too happy to be thinking about death. Let us not waste any more time imagining the words that could have been inscribed on many of these ancient headstones, but enter the church, ostensibly to look at the plaques but in reality to waylay the reverend gentleman on his way out.'

On entering the church we watched the Vicar leading the two women up the central aisle, then pausing by an ornate pulpit to point out various positions, presumably where the participants in the marriage ceremony would stand. They nodded, then followed him into the vestry while Holmes gazed at dedications inscribed on wall panels to those long gone, and I made my way towards a tomb on which a dexterously carved effigy of a knight in armour with a dog lying at his feet, caught my attention. Suddenly, in those blessedly quiet moments, Holmes roared in triumph, dragged me away from the effigy and pointed to a list of names.

'Take a close look, Watson. There is the list of ministers who have served this church from time immemorial, in fact since the church was first built.'

It meant little to me. I could see that there were two dates beside the name of each vicar, a date for the commencement of the ministry and a date for the termination, but there was one exception. Not only was the ministry recorded, but births and deaths were added in brackets, again with one exception. The odd one out was a Jonathan Williams, M.A. His ministry commenced in 1878 but the date of cessation had not been appended, nor had the year in which he died, although he was born in 1854, the same year as Holmes. The present incumbent, the Reverend Jeffrey Pyke, had joined the diocese the previous year, in 1889.

'What,' I asked Holmes, 'does this list convey that is of such interest to you?'

'Watson, you are slower than usual. Do you not see that we have discovered the identity of the man in the train?'

'You suppose, do you, that he was Jonathan Williams M.A.'

'No, Watson, I do not suppose. I know. Without doubt he is the missing man. Now let us sit and wait until the Vicar has finished with his parish duties.'

Eventually the two ladies, all smiles, emerged from the vestry with the Reverend Pyke, obviously in a hurry, in their wake.

'Good morning, gentlemen,' he said breathily, on his way to the west door.

'Good morning,' echoed Holmes as he stood up. ' You are, sir, I presume, the Reverend Jeffrey Pyke, whose name graces the list of vicars?'

The Vicar smiled, and in a rich, bass voice with lilting intonations only found in a Welshman, said it was surprising to find sightseers getting off the mark so early in the morning. Holmes explained that we were guests at Baskerville Hall, intent on tracking down the hound whose nightly howls were causing Sir Henry so much unnecessary suffering.

'You do not need to tell me who you are, gentlemen, for Sir Henry has told me often enough of the part you played, less than two years ago, in pointing the finger at a criminal intent on murder. A bad business, but undoubtedly, you saved Sir Henry's life. Needless to say, all this happened before I took up this ministry.'

'You replaced, according to the list of ministers of the parish, a certain Jonathan Williams, but someone has failed to append both the date of his termination and the date of his demise. Why is that?' asked Holmes.

The Vicar then told us that Williams vanished off the face of the earth. A sad time for his family, for the church and indeed the entire neighbourhood, because he had proved himself such a dedicated man. No one had heard a word from him since he left for a three-day holiday to stay with his sister in London. Dr Mortimer, one of the local doctors, who knew him well, thought that Williams must have suffered a nervous breakdown due to anxiety and overwork, because he was a man who had unceasingly devoted his life to the parish.

At that point I expected Holmes to enlighten the Vicar, tell him about the unnamed man on the train, if only for the sake of his wife and family, but my friend was uncharacteristically silent.

The Reverend gentleman was enormously impressed at meeting the most celebrated consulting detective in the kingdom. So much so that he invited us for lunch on the following Sunday to celebrate his first year at St Leonard's Church. Other guests would include Sir Henry, who was a regular visitor, and Sir John Falconby, the Governor of Dartmoor Prison. After graciously accepting the invitation, Holmes asked whether the Vicar had ever been called on to take services at the prison.

'Never, Mr Holmes, never. Henderson, the present chaplain, is most conscientious, rarely takes holidays and from what Sir John has told me, I gather that he spends at least fifteen minutes a week, on an individual basis, with many of the scoundrels. That, sir, is godliness.'

On hearing the church clock strike the half hour the Vicar left abruptly, already late it seemed, for a service he conducted once a week at a local school. It was then we heard a piercing whistle.

'Come on, Watson, we must have words with our irregulars.'

The street Arabs seemed dispirited, but Holmes quickly put them at their ease by explaining that he was not expecting miracles. The plain, unvarnished truth was more valuable than a dozen fictional possibilities. At times they spoke so fast that I had difficulty in following them, but Holmes seemed to get their drift immediately.

There were newcomers, we were told, including the Reverend Pyke, two farmhands in their early twenties, a milliner who came from Ilfracombe and in the height of the summer, dealers from Birmingham who sold cheap metal goods. Finally they mentioned that several months ago a florist had been approached by a man wanting to buy his business, a man who was knowledgeable about plants and flowers. That fact, for Holmes, confirmed his belief that John Stapleton, naturalist, was still living in the area.

'Watson,' ordered Holmes, in rare good humour, 'give our two young detectives a shilling each.'

Quick as lightning, Tom asked whether they would be wanted again.

'It is just possible,' said Holmes, 'so where can I contact you?'

'Joe allus knows where we is, sir. He's the barrel handler at the Lord Nelson.'

'Excellent. Now on your way, but remember,' he said, placing a finger on his lips, 'our business is secret.'

'Yes, sir. Yes, sir.' Their faces lit up. This was a day to remember.

We made steps towards the Lord Nelson. There, over a tankard of excellent local cider, we talked to an old bearded man in the far corner who looked as if he was glued to his seat. I bought him a pint, which he slurped down at an astonishing speed. Holmes gave me the nod to start chatting about the Second Afghan War. The subject always proved to be a good opener before Holmes got down to asking pertinent questions. We were in luck, for George, although we never gathered his surname, had served in Afghanistan: so too had three of his brothers, who were all killed. He lost a leg but a charitable association in the West Country had sent him to an orthopaedic surgeon who had fitted him up with a false limb.

'George,' whispered Holmes, 'tell me, do you know anything about what goes on at the prison? Are all these tales I hear about prisoners escaping true?'

'They do escape, sir, from time to time, but they usually get caught. Not much cover on these moors, you know. In fact, several years ago a criminal, a murderer he was, got gored by that ghostly hound. I had never believed the story, but I changed my mind after that.'

'Was the hound not shot?' asked Holmes.

'It might have been, but what do you believe when you hear more rumours about the beast still being heard by poachers on Sir Henry's estate? In fact, very few venture forth these days.'

'In your view is the prison well run?' I asked.

He looked puzzled. 'Why do you want to know?'

'I am a doctor and whether a man is a criminal or not I like to think that he is not left to die of some unmentionable disease.'

'The Governor there is very strict, but there have been one or two happenings like the death of the chaplain. They tried to hide it but my old mate is a warder. He tells me everything.'

'Tell us about this chaplain,' said Holmes, quite sharply.

'He was giving the last rites to a chap about to be hanged when the prisoner leapt up and throttled him. Strangled the life out of him. There was no doctor there and no one could save the poor chap.'

We left the one-legged man to his cider, and Holmes, not given to unnecessary exercise, called a cab. A long walk, I felt, would have done us the power of good, but he had something on his mind. I knew his hands were tied until he had spoken with Mycroft but he vowed that on Sunday he would change the state of play by bowling a Yorker at the opening player. By that, I presumed, he was referring to Sir John Falconby.

CHAPTER SEVEN

As we were driven back to Baskerville Hall, Holmes asked me whether, in different circumstances, I would ever have considered taking on the position as chaplain, or doctor for that matter, at Princetown. Definitely not, I told him, nor at any other prison.

He laughed. 'You would miss the ladies, Watson.'

'I would indeed.'

As we drew up in front of the crenellated towers, a red and blue kite, flying free, zoomed over the trees.

'Oh, my goodness, Holmes, young Arthur has lost his kite.'

'No, no! The child has not lost the thread. He is learning every day that with a little more string the kite will fly like a bird. A lesson to us all, Watson.'

Holmes did not wait for my comments but leapt out of the cab, making his way to the rose garden and leaving me, as usual, to deal with the driver. I knew by the speed of his movement that he was inspired in some way. Another idea had surfaced. Maybe the youngster was the inspiration?

'In an 'urry, aint 'ee, sir?' yelled the cabby.

Nodding, I paid him, then followed in the wake of Holmes, to find him conversing with Beryl Stapleton. Although still pursuing Stapleton, I knew he would never find peace of mind until he had talked with his brother, questioned the events in Whitehall and proved that treason did not have a place in Mycroft's life. He did, fortunately, have the ability to detach his mind at will from one problem in order to address the next one. For a couple of days he would be able to concentrate on the whereabouts of a murderer and the renewed threat of a legendary hound. From their conversation it was clear that Beryl Stapleton believed that her husband had some grounds for imagining he was the rightful heir to the estate. His name was Baskerville, although when they lived in York, where he was headmaster of a school, he had already changed it to that of a Dutchman. Holmes sat down on the bench beside Mrs Stapleton, probing more deeply into her husband's ancestry. She was adamant that his rightful name was Baskerville when she, as Beryl Garcia, married him in Costa Rica. It was after they had returned to England that he changed his name to Vandaleur before taking up the post as headmaster of St Olivier's private school in York.

It was during this period that he identified the Vandaleur moth that bears his name. After a serious epidemic at the school in which three boys died, the school became less and less popular, thereby much of his capital was swallowed up. He changed his name again, this time to Stapleton, before they moved south. As a naturalist he quite freely roamed the moors without anyone suspecting his foul intent. Holmes asked Mrs Stapleton whether she possessed any documentation to prove his claim to the estate. At first she thought not, then remembered that there was an old chest full of papers she had never bothered to open, let alone read. This was music to my friend's ears.

Stored in the basement at Baskerville Hall were several trunks and a considerable amount of furniture belonging to Mrs Stapleton that she might need if she ever moved away from the Hall. She had just pointed out a begrimed dark blue sea-chest when, looking quite bewildered, Baskerville appeared on the scene. Once Holmes had explained his plan of action, Sir Henry was also keen to see if Stapleton's claim on the estate had any validity in law.

With hundreds of papers spread out over the billiard table we made a systematic search through the family archive, hoping to find a definitive tree. Fortunately John Stapleton had never destroyed any papers or photographs relating to his life. His school reports from the age of seven, his degree in Botany, his sojourn in South Africa then Costa Rica, his appointment as headmaster of the school in York, but it was in the penultimate envelope, opened by Sir Henry, that we found the family tree. Stapleton was the illegitimate son of Rodger Baskerville, the younger brother of Sir Charles, who was the luckless victim of the ferocious hound. Rodger Baskerville was a libertine who had lived a dissolute life on Costa Rica before going to Brazil, where, if the reports were factual, he died of yellow fever in 1876.

John Stapleton had been christened Rodger, after his father and it was in Costa Rica that he married Beryl Garcia.

Holmes had never had any doubts about Stapleton's ancestry, not after admiring some very fine family portraits in the long hall at Baskerville Hall. Nearly two years ago, when we had first been Sir Henry's guests, we were looking at a line of portraits by fine artists, including Kneller and Reynolds. Sir Henry pointed out the wicked Sir Hugo, who had caused all the original mischief associated with the hound, a portrait of a man in a broad plumed hat, curling love-locks and white lace collar. A severe face, a brutal countenance, stern and hard set, with a coldly intolerant eye.

Later that evening, after Sir Henry had gone to his room, Holmes led me down to the banqueting-hall. With candle in hand Holmes stood on a chair, highlighting a heavily stained portrait, painted in 1647. He had said two years ago, in Baskerville's hearing, that this was the portrait of a devious man, refined but brutal, with the hint of a devil lurking in his fiercely intelligent eyes. Holding the candle up against the smoke- stained portrait, he asked me if it reminded me of anyone I knew. My immediate impulse was to suggest Sir Henry but on closer examination, I realised that it was, without doubt, the face of Stapleton. A man with designs on the succession.

The family tree from the mid-seventeenth century to the present day was the work of a fanatical man who was determined that his progeny would inherit his birthright. On the final page and under his own name he had printed the name Arthur, although at the time his wife was only three months pregnant and he had no idea whether she would give birth to a boy or a girl.

Sir Henry was mortified. He had never wanted to inherit the estate nor had he found happiness there. He had enjoyed his life farming in Canada but as the executors of the estate were unable to trace any legitimate descendents, he decided to return to England take up the mantle and provide work on his estate for the local farming community.

'Why Mr Holmes,' he cried, 'why did Stapleton never call on my great uncle to prove his right to the title? Think how much misery this distant kinsman of mine has caused.'

Mrs Stapleton shivered when she read the name of Arthur on the final page of the family tree. 'Mr Holmes,' she whispered, 'do you realise that Arthur is no longer safe? I know my husband through and through. He will not rest until he has Arthur in his clutches.'

'Rest assured, dear lady,' said Holmes in an unusually paternal manner, 'I promise you that your child will never be kidnapped.'

Baskerville turned pale. Only thirty-two years, his once handsome face now haggard with strain, he made the point that while Stapleton remained at large, his own life would be in danger. The man was a fanatic who would kill him, before willingly facing execution, in order for young Arthur to succeed to the estate.

'You will all be quite safe if you follow my dictum,' said Holmes. 'I am satisfied that Stapleton will never show his face on this estate during daylight hours. Tonight Doctor Watson and I will make every effort to trace the whereabouts of the hound, therefore I suggest, Sir Henry, that you, the child and Mrs Stapleton remain in your wing on the first floor. Palmer, the groom, will be on guard in the hall, with access to the kitchen but will make sure that all doors to the ground floor rooms are kept locked, thus ensuring your safety.

Thanking my friend, Baskerville then took Arthur by the hand to the games room, where they played trains until the child went to bed. Mrs Stapleton, who was crying, took both my hands in hers and kissed them before rushing from the room.

'Another conquest, Watson?' murmured Holmes sardonically.

'As a doctor I would say she was too emotional to utter a word. That was her way of saying thank you.'

We left Baskerville Hall as a distant clock struck midnight. There were no clouds to dim the moonlight and no wind. The very stillness was uncanny, causing us to tread softly in an attempt not to disturb foxes, wolves and barn owls that could screech as audibly as Roman geese, warning that trouble was brewing. After half an hour we stopped to take a nip of brandy. Holmes said he would dearly like to smoke his old clay pipe but the aroma of strong smelling shag tobacco might give us away.

'Why,' I asked, 'does Sir Henry not hear the creature every night?'

'Think, my dear fellow, think about young Arthur's kite.'

'Ah! Of course, it all depends on the way the wind blows.'

'That hypothesis, Watson, is correct. One that can be applied to any situation.'

At long last, softly at first, then more urgently as if running wild, we heard the creature yelp as if it had been whipped, before giving way to a frenzied, frantic barking. Immediately many other creatures were joining in the night chorus.

'Quickly,' whispered Holmes, 'we must make straight for the old barn at Merripit House.'

A few minutes later we saw the ramshackle outbuildings clearly silhouetted in the moonlight. We were only a hundred yards from the building when the baying turned to a whimper as a door was banged shut. Within seconds we heard the sound of a horse galloping in our direction. We threw ourselves on the ground behind some thick bushes but, sadly, this manoeuvre prevented us from identifying the rider. My friend, angry with himself, lit his pipe while still sitting on the ground.

'That was Stapleton,' he said, 'having just fed the beast.'

'You could have shot him, Holmes. Why did you hesitate?'

'We need him alive. The beast can be dealt with later but not until we have partaken of what I suspect to be an excellent lunch at the vicarage.'

'Holmes, as I am not a mind-reader why not explain your reasoning for keeping the man alive?'

'Too early, Watson! Much guesswork, many probabilities, but all lacking balance.'

'Again you use me but why not trust me? Even listening to one probability would not come amiss.'

'You are angry, my friend, that I can understand, but all I can say in mitigation is that this case is three-pronged. Just give this idea some thought. Who would devise a convoluted and extravagant plot to destroy me by ruining my reputation as the most famous consulting detective in the land? Who is my near equal in intellectual ability?'

'Only one person comes to mind. Your mentor before you went up to university. The man who pitted his wits against a young student, the man who wanted you to become a lieutenant in his criminal organisation, the man who controlled much of this country's underworld and who may recently have extended his operations to the Continent.'

'Yes,' barked Holmes through a cloud of smoke. 'Moriarty! Now we have to outwit him, but we will discuss our modus operandi after lunch on Sunday. In the meantime let us take a look at the beast.'

On reaching the ramshackle sheds, we could see in the moonlight that many of the slates were missing, doors were off their hinges and at the far end a wall had completely collapsed. The sound of the animal whimpering directed us towards a heavy door, recently repaired, that was fastened with an old padlock easy enough to dismantle with one shot. I suggested that as the beast had presumably been fed and watered, it would not be too dangerous to take a closer look.

'Leave the door undisturbed, Watson. Stapleton must not even suspect that we have discovered the whereabouts of his foul beast.'

'Since we have come this far, it would be interesting to get a glimpse of the animal. Could this be an ordinary hound used as a means to tempt Baskerville on to the moor, with the intention of shooting a beast that has driven him crazy for the past few months?'

'You mirror my thoughts, Watson. I intend to climb on to the roof.'

'A precarious exercise, Holmes. You will be risking life and limb. All I can say is that you have a doctor on hand.'

'It has to be done,' he said as he handed me his cape and deerstalker. Following him into the adjacent stall I lit the hurricane lamp we had brought with us, which provided enough light to distinguish several wooden boxes, barrels and rope long since discarded. Selecting the most solid boxes, we were able to build four steps, giving Holmes enough height to haul himself up on to the roof beams and through a gaping hole, on to the roof. With him he carried a length of rope and once on the roof he threw an end down to me, whereupon I tied it to the hurricane lamp, making it possible for him to haul it up. Cautiously easing himself across the roof, he lowered the lantern into the stall where the hound was incarcerated. The animal, no doubt frightened, snarled ferociously, baring its teeth as it leapt up in an effort to get at the lantern. Holmes had seen all that was needed. Much to my relief he returned to terra firma without a scratch on him.

The animal, a bloodhound, was half the size of the original beast, that may have been crossed with a mastiff. This one was grey, not black, and had not yet been covered in a cunning preparation of phosphorus to create a luminous ghostly apparition.

'This creature,' murmured Holmes, 'is a killer. In due course, when the time is ripe I will communicate with Lestrade, who must come down here to organise the local force and deal with the animal. Until then the creature's voice must be heard.'

There was something, as usual, that Holmes was not telling me. What had I missed that his brilliant mind had fathomed? Maybe all would be made plain on Sunday.....

CHAPTER EIGHT

Ten hours after we had located the beast we were sitting in Sir Henry's family pew at the rear of the nave in St Leonard's Church. Sun streamed in through the east window, highlighting a magnificent stained glass window by Burne-Jones, depicting the nativity. Baskerville told us that it was a recently acquired gift from an anonymous donor. Holmes gave a barely perceptible wink, confirming what I had already guessed. Sir Henry was the benefactor.

With the choir in such excellent voice, the trebles' high-pitched sounds echoed around the church. During these periods I noticed that Holmes had his eyes closed, making sure that nothing distracted him from enjoying such flawless singing. His eyes were open, however, when Sir John Falconby slipped quietly into his pew as the Reverend Pyke began his exhortation. A lady sitting alongside him was wearing a brightly coloured turquoise hat – more French than English- whom I imagined to be his wife.

'Falconby invariably arrives late,' whispered Baskerville, who was sitting on my right. 'Too many problems to deal with at the prison. He needs another deputy.'

The Governor of Dartmoor prison, an austere looking fellow who was as lean and as tall as Holmes but without the sharp features, gave a slight nod in our direction.

'A signal,' said Baskerville, to Holmes, 'that he will be staying for lunch.'

A slight smile from my friend, who became noticeably relaxed. One step nearer to meeting his brother, provided he was dealt the right cards.

The short sermon, taken from St Mathew's gospel, was based on the parable of the tares. Reverend Pyke expounded on the kingdom of heaven being likened unto a man who sowed good seed in his field, but while he slept his enemy came and sowed tares among the wheat. He concluded by saying that the field is the world; the good seed are the children of the kingdom but the tares are the children of the wicked one and the enemy who sowed them is the devil.

'Moriarty,' mouthed Holmes.

At the conclusion of the service we remained seated while the congregation left to the stirring music of Handel. In my notes I forgot to name the work, but that omission will have to be forgiven. It is, of course, not important, because Holmes gave orders for the notes on the case to be deposited in my old sea-chest at the bank. I am hoping, devoutly, that if he solves both cases satisfactorily he will change his mind.

Sir John Falconby joined us outside the church where Sir Henry introduced us. It was quite apparent from Sir John's reaction that he had no idea Holmes was staying at Baskerville Hall, let alone having lunch at the vicarage. As Pyke joined us, having divested himself of his robes, Sir John said, 'We have met before, Mr Holmes, under very different circumstances.'

'You must remind me, sir, for my mind has no need to record past cases. My own Boswell standing beside me, is an excellent amanuensis.'

'You, sir, were Homer. I was Falcon.'

'Of course, my dear chap. Our university days, when boxing was a sport to be recommended. You certainly

87

thrashed me, Falconby, but did I not take my revenge for that savage blow below the belt?'

'Touché,' laughed his opponent. 'We later crossed swords or was it épées, in the gymnasium, when your thrusts proved more powerful than mine. Nowadays all I play is chess.'

'Then I will join you in combat,' retorted Holmes, without giving the matter a second's thought.

'That,' remarked Falconby, 'is an opening gambit.'

The Governor was a highly intelligent and astute individual. The moment he had set eyes on Holmes he knew the game was on. He was throwing down the gauntlet. Not at all the draconian chap we had expected to meet.

Following in our host's wake, we walked across the lawn, all set for a game of croquet, towards the front door of the vicarage. Holmes halted our progress to enquire of Pyke whether the mole hills on the lawn were, in a game of croquet, accepted as a hazard and if so, did one score an additional point for dexterity in avoiding them.

'You must ask my wife, Mr Holmes, for I never play the game but I am fully aware that our gardener cannot come to terms with the little fellows. They outwit him at every turn.'

Mrs Pyke, the lady I had seen in the church wearing the turquoise chapeau, was in the hall to welcome us. I had indeed jumped to conclusions imagining her to be Sir John's wife, but I was most assuredly correct in one fact. Her outfit, as we later discovered, had been purchased in Paris when she and her husband were on holiday.

Many topics were discussed over an excellent lunch but Holmes ate sparingly, being more interested in the conversation than in the perfectly prepared pheasant that had obviously been allowed to hang for at least three days. At one stage, when we were all mellow from the effects of an unexceptionably fine claret, he asked Falconby whether, being in such an outlandish spot, he had difficulty in attracting reliable officers and warders.

'None whatsoever,' replied Falconby. 'Princeton, no longer outlandish, is a growing community where the warders and their families live quite happily. There were and still are, many men in these parts who risk their lives working in the tin mines, strong men who now prefer to work above ground in fresh air.'

'That I can understand, but what attracts clerks, doctors and chaplains, especially after the murderous attack on a chaplain less than two years ago?'

'The Reverend Butterworth, unfortunately, brought it upon himself by telling Corton, the convict who killed him, that the convict's wife had just given birth to a healthy child. Corton had been under lock and key for twelve months. Butterworth should have given the matter more thought.'

'Difficult, I would have thought,' said Holmes, 'to have filled his place.'

'Luck was on my side. Nearly eighteen months ago when, here in St Leonard's Church attending morning service, I found myself sitting alongside a man of the cloth. During the service we exchanged pleasantries. After the service, whilst we strolled in the churchyard, I told him that the prison had been without a chaplain for three months. Three months during which time those criminals repenting of their sins had received no moral support. The Lord above must have had me in his sights that day because Henderson said he would be prepared to help out for a few weeks while he looked around in the West Country for another living. Those few weeks, thank the Lord above, have become months and hopefully Henderson will remain at the prison for many years to come.'

'What exactly was he doing down here?' I asked.

'A sad life, doctor. He had been living a happily married life in a good benefice in Manchester when his young wife died giving birth to their first child. After that he had to escape. A natural reaction, but however far one runs there is no escape from memories. They remain to haunt us.'

'Did you take up references?' queried Holmes.

'No need. One does not reach the rank of Colonel without being an excellent judge of character, as anyone who worked for me in Whitehall will tell you.'

'Whitehall?' queried Holmes.

'Yes, on special duties for the Home Office during the riots.'

Holmes looked in my direction, his eyes gleaming. I knew what he was thinking. Falconby and Mycroft's paths could have crossed.

'Henderson,' said Falconby, as if trying to justify the lack of a reference, 'drives himself too far. He makes a point of spending fifteen minutes every week with any of the men who wish to see him. I have to tell you that the list increases daily. He refuses to take holidays which, to my mind, is a great mistake, but on the other hand he is an accomplished horseman, spending at least an hour a day in the saddle.'

Mycroft's name had not been uttered but Falconby and Holmes, or Falcon and Homer, understood each other perfectly. There was also an underlying current in my friend's questions, but quite what he was shooting at was, at the time, beyond me.

After we had finished our coffees Mrs Pyke said she needed advice on roses planted by the gardener earlier in the year that were not responding to tea leaves and natural manure. Holmes had little interest in botany unless it was directly linked to poison. The only idea in his mind at that moment was to pin Falconby down to that promised game of chess, so Baskerville gave me a nod, and we left them in close combat. Following Mrs Pyke, we made our way towards a bed of tired looking bush roses with drooping heads and yellowing leaves.

'Dear madam,' said Baskerville, keeping a straight face, 'do you give them Indian or China tea?'

'Don't joke, Sir Henry, this is a serious business. Tea leaves provide valuable nutrition.'

'Of course, my dear lady, but I would suggest that the manure may be too strong. A little goes a long way.'

'You could be right,' she said after considerable thought.

Meanwhile, during our sortie into the garden, Holmes was invited to Dartmoor on the following day for a game of chess in the Governor's office. A game, I prayed, that would, one day, end in checkmate.

CHAPTER NINE

Baskerville, who had been agreeably surprised at seeing another aspect of Sir John's character, suggested we take either the wagonette or the trap to the prison. The weather looking unsettled, we elected to use the wagonette. Lose no time, Sir Henry had said, strike while the iron is hot. Holmes needed no telling.

Guards, who were on duty at the main gate, had been notified of our arrival and had been given orders to take us straight up to the Governor's quarters. His office was a large room on the first floor with windows on two sides. The view to the south overlooked the compound; to the north a vast barren vista of moorland, crags and in the distance, great tors.

Ivory chessmen were set up on a table near the window overlooking the moorland. Falconby invited me to take a comfortable chair while the combatants sat on two hard chairs vis-à-vis. This game of chess was like no other. Falconby began by picking up the white king. 'Let us suppose,' he said slowly, 'that this is not a white king but an innocent piece in a wider game. The black king's pawn has already made an opening gambit quite against the spirit and ethic of the game.'

Holmes nodded. 'Your supposition, Falcon, cannot be faulted, which is why the white knight and the white bishop have to protect their king from the evil machinations of the notorious black king who is aided by his lieutenants, mere pawns in the game.'

'The white queen too, Homer, is under fire. Literally and metaphorically. Six attempts on her life. Let us pray there are no more.'

What on earth was Falconby talking about? Surely he could not be referring to attempts on the life of Victoria Regina? I was at a loss, but gave up speculating in an effort not to lose the thread.

'The Bohemians,' said the Governor, 'have undoubtedly raised the expectations of this game. Dobrusky has demonstrated a method of attack in which the black king can be checkmated in four, even three moves.'

'I intend,' said Holmes as he castled, 'to double-check this villainous piece.'

'Castling is no answer, Homer. You have left the white king in a tight corner.'

'A tight corner can act as a magnet. Draw the enemy fire.'

'In normal circumstances,' said Falconby, replacing the white queen, 'one would expect this piece to be out of danger but I suspect the enemy is within. For the present we know that the black king, whoever he is, has the advantage, and we must never forget that the French call the bishop the *fou*.'

'In other words,' laughed Holmes, 'a jester who has many tricks up his sleeve, but believe me, Falcon, a dirty game can be overcome by changing the pattern of evil moves, check and checkmate before the colour of the mole within has become apparent.'

It was not quite clear to me what Holmes was driving at, other than he intended to go straight in for the kill.

93

'Homer,' said the Governor, looking him straight in the face, 'I would trust the white king with my life. Now it is up to you to prolong the game long enough to save the life of someone who has achieved so much, in a phlegmatic and restrained style, for the British Empire.'

They shook hands in silence. Holmes rose, crossed the room and looking into the compound, nodded to himself as if he had just solved a difficult and obscure theorem. Mycroft had not once been mentioned, therefore the secrecy of the realm had not been breached. Holmes now knew he had carte blanche to proceed further, but neither of us had been expecting the next move.

'Doctor Watson,' said Falconby quite sharply, now looking as austere as the first time I had set eyes upon him.

'Yes, Sir John?'

'We have a sick prisoner needing immediate attention but, unfortunately, the prison doctor is not available this morning. In the circumstances I wondered whether you would care to make a diagnosis?'

Holmes, quoting from the Bard, roared, 'Stand not upon the order of your going, Watson, but go at once. Just leave us to exchange anecdotes about university days.'

A warder led the way towards the cell in which Mycroft had been kept in solitary confinement for nearly two weeks.

'Ee's ill, doctor, and ee's not ill,' said the warder, 'if you know what I mean.'

'No I do not, so you had better explain.'

'Lost an awful lot of weight, never says a word when 'is food is given him, almost as though ee's a mute. On the other hand, the chaplain sees him every day, meaning summat is up. It makes me think the prisoner might be dying and trying to make his peace with the Almighty for the evil crimes 'ee has committed.'

'What evil crimes?'

'All very secret,' said the warder, tapping his nose, 'but everyone here knows that it is a wicked crime against the Crown.'

'Does he talk to the chaplain?'

'Don't think 'ee ever says a word. It's like the chaplain's waiting for him to die. If 'ee does the hangman will lose a few pence and that'll give us all a good laugh. Talk of the devil,' he said, sotto voce, as the Reverend Henderson emerged from Mycroft's cell. The chaplain, looking in our direction, realising that there was no need to lock the door, gave us a brief wave, turned smartly on his heels and walked slowly in the opposite direction. The warder then asked me whether I wanted him to remain in the cell.

'No, my good man, you have been most communicative, told me all I need to know.'

'Very well, sir, I will stay outside the door. Just call me if you need me.'

Mycroft, whose eyes were closed, was lying on a mattress on the floor. He could have been asleep but I waited until the door clanged shut behind me before getting down on my knees to take a closer look. He had certainly lost weight and by the pallor of his skin, hope as well.

'Mycroft,' I whispered, 'listen to me.'

His whole frame shuddered then he opened his eyes. 'Watson' he gasped, 'I thought it was a dream, no, a nightmare. How on earth did you...................'

'Relax and listen. Your brother is here playing a bizarre game of chess with Falconby in which they are discussing future moves against a criminal black king on behalf of an innocent white king.'

'That makes sense,' whispered Mycroft, 'because Falconby says he believes in my innocence but knows there is no way to prove it. He has made it clear that I will not be charged with high treason immediately because the state of affairs in the capital, and in the country at large, is damaging the monarchy. That is why I desperately need to talk to my brother in an effort to forestall more riots.'

'It is patently obvious, Mycroft, that the Governor cannot possibly allow you to have direct contact with your brother. I suggest you confide in me.'

'You might then become embroiled in a dastardly plot and I have no intention of placing your life in jeopardy.'

'Have you discussed the matter with the chaplain?'

'Never! I allow him to do the talking. He visits me every day, sometimes twice. I let him talk, I let him pray but as for a confession, nothing doing, because I have the feeling that someone in the Foreign Office, maybe even the Minister, is paying him to probe, to dig deep. Could be my imagination. Circumstances like these can affect one's reasoning, but I assure you, Watson, there is nothing wrong with my mental state, although, as you can see, I have lost weight. Not a bad thing really, easier for the hangman to carry out his business.'

Before I could persuade him not to give in so easily, even in jest, there was a knock at the door, giving me just enough time to place my hand on Mycroft's brow before the warder entered the cell.

'You all right, sir?'

'Yes, but I do need a few more minutes to complete my examination.'

'Yes, sir.' Once again he banged the door, leaving us a few minutes grace.

Mycroft whispered urgently, 'Make Falconby believe that my memory is faulty; tell him incarceration has affected my mind, but I must see my brother, only he can deal with this problem. Make sure you tell him to enquire into the business of the Hanover Club.'

Hanover Club failed to ring a bell with me, however, promising to do what I could, but feeling totally inadequate, I returned to the Governor's office where Falconby was waiting impatiently.

'Well, doctor, what is your diagnosis?'

'Two weeks incarceration has affected his mind. I do not mean that he is mad in the accepted sense of the word, only that his memory is faulty. He also believes that the Chaplain is there not to comfort him, but to question him.'

Falconby poured scorn on the idea. He said it was a normal reaction until prisoners eventually realised the chaplain was on their side. He was a devoted, god-fearing man who wanted the men to confess their sins in order to pray for forgiveness. In so many cases it worked in helping anguished souls to find peace. Falconby, did, however, make it clear that Mycroft's mental state was not good news, for in two weeks time officers from Scotland Yard would be down to question him again. 'Gentlemen,' he said slowly, 'how does one treat the mind?'

'There is a new science emerging,' replied Holmes, 'but it is too early, perhaps, to be used in soothing the mental state of my brother. Maybe I should see him? Pacify him and get to the truth about what happened immediately prior to his arrest?'

'Not possible, I am afraid. My instructions are quite clear. Under no circumstances can you be allowed access to him. I am truly sorry, Homer, my hands are tied, but I am eager to hear more about this emerging science.'

Holmes clasped his hands together, then frowned as if trying to remember a name. This, I knew was an opening gambit. At last he said, 'There is a fellow in Austria, my age, a neurologist called Freud, who for six years experimented in the Institute of Cerebral Anatomy in Vienna. More recently he has been studying symptoms of hysteria and by using hypnosis, a cathartic method in my view, he has produced results.'

'Vienna is not the answer, Homer.'

'No, but there are neurologists in London who studied with him in Vienna.'

As Holmes turned towards the window, ostensibly to find inspiration, he gave me a slight nod. Not really understanding what my friend was intending I had a fit of coughing while trying to work out what was needed. At last it became clear. 'Holmes, you are right, you do not need Vienna, not if this fellow Freud has associates in London.'

'Of course, Watson! I will telegraph Dr Breucot, who is an associate member at my club. Tell him the matter is urgent and get him down here tomorrow. Sir Henry, I know, will welcome another guest.'

Falconby looked quite taken aback. 'I am quite sure that neither the Home Office nor the Foreign Office would look favourably on a stranger hearing the inside story. It is highly secret. Think of the damage to this country if this comparatively unknown neurologist talks to the Press.'

I was quick off the mark. 'All doctors, Sir John, respect confidences in the same manner as a priest.'

'Very well,' he said grudgingly. 'Get the fellow down here. The examination must take place here in my office, enabling me to be party to the entire exchange.'

'An excellent, idea,' smiled Holmes, 'Excellent, my dear fellow.'

On our return to Baskerville Hall we stopped in Tavistock. Holmes asked me to spend time in the Lord Nelson listening to the old man in the corner while he went in search of his two young irregulars. He needed them, he said, to carry out a clandestine mission. At the time I had not the vaguest idea what was in his mind.

As soon as we continued our journey he asked me what I truly thought about Mycroft's health.

'He has lost weight and is under no illusion about his fate, although he still has a vestige of faith in his younger brother. Mycroft implored me to make sure that Falconby is made aware of his mental state, but you can rest assured, Holmes, that there is nothing wrong with him; he has lost none of his brain power. I have the feeling that he does not trust the chaplain, who is acting as a grand inquisitor.'

'Nor is he,' growled Holmes, 'expecting forgiveness for sins he has not committed?'

'Will this Dr Breucot pass muster?'

'Without doubt, my dear friend. His English is excellent.'

I was doubtful. 'How can we be sure that he will cancel important appointments in London tomorrow?'

'From what I know of the man he champions freedom and justice. Take it from me, Watson, he will leave Paddington on the early train and hare for the prison at breakneck speed.'

'Holmes, have you ever heard of the Hanover Club?'

'No! Is this pertinent to the case?'

'It may be. I have no idea whether it is situated in Hanover Square or elsewhere in the capital, but according to Mycroft it needs to be investigated.'

'You know, Watson, as I have said before, if the art of detection begins and ends in reasoning, my brother could sit comfortably in an armchair and prove to be the greatest criminal agent of all time. Hanover suggests to me that he already suspects which way the wind is blowing. A little more cord and the kite can fly even higher.

As soon as Dr Breucot has had words with my brother I too will travel to the *Great Wen* in an effort to seek out the Hanover Club. You will remain at the Hall, making sure that Baskerville is safe from attack, although I am of the opinion that murder is not contemplated in the immediate future.'

'What gives you that idea? What clues have I missed and what have you not told me, Holmes?'

'The clues are mixed like those lights in an acrostic. They need deciphering. Tonight, Watson, I suggest we make another sortie in the direction of the Merripit barns, but this time we will be in position soon after dinner?'

'With what object, Holmes?'

'To discover from which direction the mysterious rider approaches.'

By ten o'clock we were in a position of vantage amidst thick bushes, where Holmes was able to smoke his strong smelling shag. For over an hour we sat waiting on a massive oak log hidden, I imagine, until a peasant could remove it safely without being caught in the act. Holmes asked me what I made of Falconby. All I could say was that I saw no fault in the man. Charged with an onerous duty, he was obeying the letter of the law. If he had been given orders not to allow Holmes access to his brother he had carried out the injunction, but had gone out of his way to address the situation over a bizarre game of chess. I admired the man for his ingenuity.

'Ingenuity! Not a talent I would ascribe to a man who takes on staff without references.'

'You have the chaplain in mind, the Reverend Henderson?'

'I most certainly have.'

'He certainly persists in visiting Mycroft every day. Surely one cannot fault him for interrogating your brother? After all, he might come across just one fact that would prove his innocence.'

'Watson, do you not see, that he has to prove Mycroft's guilt beyond a shadow of doubt in order to cast the limelight on someone else. We have to trace the villain whose heinous stratagems go far beyond the incarceration of one man. I believe that once Dr Breucot has talked with Mycroft we can glean enough information to enable us to pursue the man, capture him and see him hanged.'

At last we heard a horse galloping across the moor. Not from the north as I expected, but from the south, travelling around the infamous Grimpen Mire, where animals losing their footing often get sucked into a treacherous slough. The wretched beast in the barn also heard the approaching rider. It reacted by howling, then barking, as it hurled itself against the door in an effort to escape. Within minutes the rider appeared. Dismounting, he yelled out to the beast to quieten down, effective because the barking soon became a miserable whimper. It was difficult to see what was happening but we clearly heard the sound of a bucket being dropped into a well.

A few minutes later the rider unlocked the barn door, then threw something on the floor, presumably food, before carrying the bucket of water inside. About ten minutes later the rider, whom we could not distinguish, dragged the animal out on a long cord, encouraging it to bark ferociously.

Half an hour later the hound was returned to the barn, where it quietened down. Although we heard the man shouting it was impossible to hear what he actually said to the animal. Soon after midnight the rider made a speedy departure. Once he was out of earshot we returned to the Hall, now knowing that the animal was always fed and watered around midnight.

Before turning in for the night, Holmes surprised me by saying that he wanted me to be at the prison in the morning, in time to welcome Dr Breucot. He felt it would be more diplomatic if he kept well clear, leaving Falconby to do his job, but he did stress that it would be an advantage if I sat in the outer room in the event that Dr Breucot needed assistance. Why, I wondered, as I dropped off, would a first-rate neurologist need the assistance of a commonplace doctor!

CHAPTER TEN

Palmer, Sir Henry's groom, who had a sister living in Princetown, drove the wagonette to the prison, where he dropped me off before making for his sister's home, where he planned to spend the morning. Her husband was a warder in the prison, so en route Palmer was able to give me an insight into how prisoners managed to survive such hard and inhuman treatment.

A young, clean looking warder took me up to the Governor's office on the first floor. Falconby was surprised Holmes had not accompanied me, but I could see that he was relieved and pleased that his old opponent had seen fit to observe the proprieties of the situation. He was intent on hearing exactly what Mycroft had said to me during my previous visit. Was there anything I had omitted to mention?

There was nothing new. I repeated what he had already been told about Mycroft not appreciating the constant questioning he had to endure during the chaplain's visits. Falconby let that pass. Changing the subject, he said that he was looking forward to Dr Breucot's visit because new methods might be the answer to future problems. I suggested that once Breucot arrived and I had made the introductions it might be a good idea if I sat in the outer room until he had finished his examination. I would then be on call if Mycroft needed the assistance of another doctor. Nodding, Falconby smiled, opening his hands in an expansive gesture. He was a man at ease with himself.

The young warder appeared again. This time he was followed by Dr Breucot, a tall, bearded fellow wearing spectacles, who limped into Falconby's office. I shook his hand whilst explaining that it was Holmes who had telegraphed him but, as protocol prevented the well-known consulting detective from being present, I would support him, and after his prognosis we would make our way to Baskerville Hall. He thanked me in a guttural Austrian accent, although I have to say his English was excellent. I then introduced him to Falconby, who welcomed his support in a difficult case but at the same time made it clear he had to hear every word the prisoner uttered. The safety of the kingdom was paramount.

Breucot, in quite a peremptory manner, said he had dealt with similar cases in the past and that if he discussed his patients' ailments he would soon be ostracised. With the ground rules laid down the two men talked amicably about the problems loss of privilege can cause in the mind, until Mycroft, supported by two warders, appeared on the scene. His skin, a ghastly shade of yellow, made him look jaundiced, and although he had lost considerable weight he was still a hefty man. As he entered he looked at Dr Breucot and grimaced, before closing his eyes with a strange smile on his face. At that point I quietly left the room to sit alone in the outer office, and of course, to eavesdrop.

Dr Breucot's accent was no bar to hearing every word he uttered, and every question that he asked relating to Mycroft's sleep patterns, but the answers were inaudible. Disappointing, maddening even, because I had nothing to report to Holmes.

Suddenly there came the sound of a heavy thud in Falconby's office. I knew instantly that Mycroft had collapsed. Had my diagnosis been totally off course? What had I missed? A worried Falconby opened the door, imploring me to help Dr Breucot deal with the problem. Maybe inviting a neurologist to examine a prisoner was a procedure outside the realms of the Home Office, not sanctioned, therefore unacceptable?

Falconby and I lifted Mycroft, who was still some weight, back on to the armchair, while Dr Breucot pushed another arm chair under his legs, producing a make-shift bed. Bending over him, I listened to his steady breathing. It was quite normal. Then I took his pulse, that too was normal. There was no cause, as far as I could see, for this sudden collapse.

At that moment a cacophony of sound broke out, reverberating around the compound below us. Sirens going full blast, followed by piercing whistles in the prison, and hooters in the distance.

'You must excuse me, gentlemen,' yelled an angry Falconby, 'Another prisoner has escaped. These occurrences have to be dealt with immediately. I am relying on you, Dr Watson, to make sure that this prisoner does not die, thus carrying important information with him to the grave.'

No one could have been more surprised than I at the turn of events, although the years I had spent with Holmes should have prepared me for such a charade. It should have been crystal clear.

'Quickly, Watson, we have not a moment to lose,' said the Austrian doctor in an all too familiar voice.

There is no doubt that Holmes should have been an actor. As I have mentioned before, he would not have been out of place in Sir Henry Irving's company at the Lyceum. Of all his accents and disguises, Breucot was the most compelling.

Mycroft opened his eyes. 'Well done, brother, he said clearly, 'but we have so little time. You must learn exactly what happened on the night I was arrested.'

'Go ahead. Watson will take notes.'

'It happened on a Tuesday night three weeks ago. After a short spell at the Diogenes Club, where I enjoyed a meal in silence, I made my way to the office. I had the feeling that one of the members followed me into Whitehall but never saw his face. The night watchman let me into the building, although I do have my own keys for emergencies. As I climbed the stairs to my office I felt that there was someone watching me, but saw no one. However, I took the precaution of locking my office door. My purpose that night was to continue auditing the accounts of the British Embassy in St Petersburg, where inordinate and unexplained payments were being made to the consulate in Dresden. This I believe, though have not yet proved, relates to the business of Wilhelm II, who made three visits to Britain in the past year, including Balmoral, Windsor, and Buckingham Palace.

The file is kept under lock and key in a burglar-proof cabinet, yet when sorting through a vast amalgamation of papers, to which only I am privy, I came across reports relating to both the Cleveland Street Brothel Scandal and the Ripper murders which are more damaging to the monarchy than you can possibly imagine. It is rumoured that Eddy, the Duke of Clarence, was patronising the brothel. His name is again linked with the Ripper Case. In the documents were the names of the five prostitutes who were murdered, the secret marriage of a young royal prince and the involvement of an artist called Sickert. The case, as you know, was handled by Aberline, but neither the Press nor the public heard the true facts.

The girls, according to the documents, were murdered in a ritual way related to methods possibly used by the top rank of masons, but whoever carried out the murders must have been a practised medical man who may have wanted to damage the image of the masons, many of whom are god-fearing and worthy men. Sir William Gull, who was discovered with blood on his clothing, must have examined the corpses, but whatever the truth of the matter, I had to get rid of the papers. The embers in the hearth were still glowing, and as there was only one way in which I could protect the monarchy, the papers had to be burnt. I was sorting through them when I came across twenty or thirty leaflets exhorting the populace to rise, march to Buckingham Palace on the succeeding Sunday in a well-organised plot designed to get rid of the monarchy and follow in the footsteps of the French by creating a republic.'

At that point the sirens went off again.

'Quickly, brother,' urged Holmes, 'tell me about the Hanover Club, we may not have much more time.'

'Ah! The Hanover Club, hypothetical, perhaps, but I truly believe that money is being transferred from the coffers in St Petersburg to Dresden to finance a club that has only one objective, but what you need to find, brother, is the mastermind. It is patently obvious to me that there are spies in the embassy, the consulate and an insider in the Home Office, all working to one end. Strange to say, the Hanover Club is a fairly recent establishment, in fact I heard two fellows talking about it when I was last in the Diogenes.'

We heard someone ascending the stairs.

'Quickly, brother, what did you do with the papers?'

'I managed to burn all the Ripper material but not the leaflets, before six officers, who must have been lying in wait, broke down the door and arrested me.'

Mycroft closed his eyes as the Governor entered. 'That,' said Falconby savagely, was a false alarm and when I lay hands on the culprits, they will wish that they had never been born. I guarantee they will never play the same trick again.'

Mycroft opened his eyes. 'I am sorry,' he said, looking at Holmes, 'but you did not give me your name.'

'It is of no importance,' said the Austrian doctor, looking distinctly Jewish. 'I am here to help you remember the past few months.'

'Memory is a strange asset,' murmured Mycroft. 'I can tell you what I did at school, and much about my younger brother, but the immediate past is a blank.'

Falconby, suddenly looking pleased, relaxed. What had Mycroft said? Nothing important, other than the immediate past was a blank.

Dr Breucot moved the armchair on which Mycroft's legs rested, and sat down.

'The prisoner,' he said to Falconby, 'will continue to suffer from this affliction. There is little that hypnosis will achieve.'

The Governor was effusive in thanking the Austrian neurologist. Mycroft, who still looked comatose, gave me a broad wink as I bent over him to feel his pulse once again.

'This man,' I said, looking Falconby straight in the face, 'should be kept in the prison hospital for a few days. Give him a book to read, but no questions which would undoubtedly raise his blood pressure.'

'You are in one accord with the prison doctor who also recommended similar treatment simply because he could not isolate the symptoms.'

Mycroft groaned, before asking softly whether he was in heaven.

'No, you are not,' snapped Falconby, 'but thanks to the two gentlemen here you will be kept in comfortable quarters for a few days.'

As we were about to leave Mycroft sat bolt upright, waving his arms around and pointing at Falconby. 'I know you, do I not? We met at the Foreign Office after that Steiffel affair.'

'He really is a mental case,' shouted Falconby. 'I will have him certified.'

'A great mistake, in my view,' said Dr Breucot. 'He has obviously mistaken you for someone else. That does not mean he is mad.'

'Yes,' laughed Falconby uneasily, 'you could be right.'

Mycroft clapped his hands before falling back into a supine position with, I must say, a wicked grin on his face.

On our return to the Hall I mentioned how fortuitous and well-timed the alarm signals had been.

'Fortuitous? No!' emphasised Holmes. 'Well-timed, you could say. A little planning, Watson, is all it takes. Those two irregulars did a splendid job by chasing across the moor yelling at each other in the hearing of the guards. All they had to shriek was *there he goes, there he goes, let's catch him.* Only eight or nine words were needed to create the furore that ensued.'

Holmes could always pit his wits against impossible circumstances. Who could possibly have forecast that he would have had words with his brother in the Governor's own office? What a pity he had not been in Afghanistan where such diversions, caused by a simple action, would have been welcomed.

We broke our journey at Tavistock, where Tom and Josh were waiting behind the Lord Nelson. I gave them a shilling each. Holmes, tapping his nose, told them that we might need their assistance again but warned them that such actions were highly secret.

'Yes, Mr Holmes,' they cried in unison, their eyes sparkling. Waving us goodbye, they watched us clamber into the wagonette. 'Constables of the future,' I murmured.

CHAPTER ELEVEN

On our return to Baskerville Hall we called at the telegraph office in Tavistock, far quicker than continuing to Grimpen, in order for Holmes to telegraph Lestrade, asking for his assistance in capturing a man who was keeping a wild beast in captivity, a man whom he believed to be Stapleton.

'Why Lestrade, Holmes, when there are capable officers on the spot?'

'His net is wide, Watson, and from the experience he gained two years ago he would be of great assistance in nailing this fellow. Sir Henry and his household still need constant protection from a vicious beast, so too do the night shepherds and moor-land farmers. I have no doubt, that if Lestrade accepts the challenge, he will first of all call at Ross and Mangles in the Fulham Road.'

'Ah! The dealers who, three years ago, sold the strongest and most savage dog in their possession to a stranger? This dog, Holmes, although smaller, could well be a bull-mastiff but it has not yet been smothered in phosphorus.'

'It was a stroke of genius using artificial means to change an ordinary dog into a ghostly luminous beast. An opponent I would welcome at the end of my foil, but what I need to know, most urgently, is whether he returned to London in his present guise.'

'His present guise!' I was staggered. 'You know, Holmes?'

'A deduction, Watson.'

'Holmes,' I said wrathfully, 'I do not, as a rule, have second sight.'

'No, Watson, no, but like any theorem there is much to be proved. Think about the legend. The first legendary hound, we are told, ripped out the throat of Sir Hugo Baskerville, but Stapleton knew his beast did not have to go that far. The very sight of the animal terrified Sir Charles, causing the death of an old man with a weak heart, making it impossible to prove the guilt of a man who, with malice aforethought, had perpetrated murder without ever having to lay hands on the victim. The present creature, maybe half the size, is being trained, nevertheless, to achieve the same object. It is undeniably savage and its howling equally terrifying, although it no longer has quite the same impact on Sir Henry now that he realises we can all hear the creature.'

A few days after our arrival Sir Henry had become a changed man. No longer looking depressed and jaundiced, he laughed and joked with Beryl as they walked round the rose-garden. He played with young Arthur and was even teaching the two-year old child to read. Not only that, but Arthur now knew the names of all the people depicted in the portraits hanging in the rather forbidding Great Hall. One, however, was missing.

It was the portrait that Holmes had pointed out to me shortly after the convict, Selden, had crashed to his death on the rocks when fleeing from the beast. The portrait of a devious, brutal man with a devil lurking in his cruelly intelligent eyes. The face of Stapleton had sprung out of that canvas. At the time reincarnation came to mind, but it was evidence that Stapleton was a Baskerville. No doubt about it.

Lestrade, who had met Sir Henry on his last visit to Baskerville Hall, felt strangely drawn to the baronet, who had no airs and graces, a man who preferred a quiet life

113

farming in Canada but one who had accepted that running the estate was a duty he owed the families who had been dependent on the estate for several generations. Before Lestrade's arrival Holmes, knowing it would jeopardise the inspector's future if he remained on the scene, asked Sir Henry to welcome him. The Scotland Yard man, he had said, was a stout fellow but while Mycroft was still suspected of high treason, compromising the Inspector in a case concerning the Crown would be unforgivable.

Baskerville understood the problem. Holmes went on to explain that he had a few matters to resolve before returning to London in a day or two, but one of us would remain at Baskerville Hall until Stapleton had been apprehended. He had no need to ask me whether I wished to remain because he knew that I too was intent both on snaring Stapleton and proving Mycroft's innocence.

'Holmes,' the baronet said softly, 'if you succeed in drawing a noose round the neck of this evil fellow I shall be forever in your debt. Beryl and young Arthur mean so much to me. Our lives will be happier; we can begin life again.'

Holmes nodded, knowing exactly what Baskerville was implying.

We were interrupted by Beryl running into the room with a telegraph in hand for Holmes. For one awful moment I thought that Lestrade must be calling off the action, but the face of my friend lit up.

'Watson, thanks to Lestrade the case of the dead chimney sweep can no longer be considered a failure. The Inspector arrested that Indian Thug as he was boarding a ship to escape justice.'

Baskerville, who had no idea what Holmes was talking about, was curious indeed, and on hearing about the successful outcome of a bizarre case, he congratulated us both.

Holmes then went on to extol the virtues of Inspector Lestrade, an excellent chap, who would be arriving at Tavistock on an early train the following morning. He also mentioned that after breakfast he would take another look at St Leonard's church, perhaps chat with the verger followed by a pint with the old man in the corner at the Lord Nelson who is a fount of knowledge.

I knew there was more to the visit than gazing at Gothic arches and a list of past and present clergy, but what would the verger know that the Vicar had not been able to tell us?

No carrot had been needed in luring Lestrade to Devonshire. He always maintained it was a relief to escape the stench and fog of the Great Wen. We knew he would call at the County Constabulary to enlist the assistance of several men in the hope that they would be prepared to give up their evening's leisure to hunt for the hound. Much more exhilarating than playing darts in the local.

Sir Henry was also keen to join in the hunt but Holmes, before leaving, advised him to stay in the house with Beryl, young Arthur and servants who must be within call. Neither Baskerville nor I understood why this was necessary, but ruefully the baronet agreed.

Holmes departed after breakfast but my notes about the way in which my friend spent the rest of the day are almost illegible. Fortunately, I have a good memory. On arriving in Tavistock he spent some time looking for the irregulars. At last he found Josh cleaning out a pigsty behind The Lord Nelson. Anything in Josh's view was better than swilling out pigsties, so hurriedly finishing the job, he followed Holmes in the direction of the church. His task was to find out whether the Vicar was in the vicinity and the whereabouts of the verger. In less than ten minutes his task was accomplished. The Vicar, whom Holmes did not wish to see, was visiting a sick parishioner and the verger was in the vestry. Holmes told Josh to remain in the churchyard, keep an eye on the lichgate and whistle if anyone approached the church.

The verger who, by the time Holmes entered, was cleaning the brass eagle which served as a lectern, was surprised that so eminent a man had come to ask his opinion. The questions were nearly all centred on one man. Henderson. First of all, was there any gossip surrounding him? Did he frequent the town, and if so was he on his own? Did he ride carrying a shotgun and did he aid the Vicar in any way?

In less than an hour the verger who, in Holmes's opinion, had missed his profession by not writing a scandal column in the local paper, was able to provide an authentic background for the prison chaplain.

Several times a week Henderson could be found in The Lord Nelson, chatting to the old man in the corner who, after he had imbibed a few, gave him all the latest news.

The Chaplain showed scant interest in town matters but was always agog to know what was happening at Baskerville Hall. When Beryl shopped in the market he was never far away, watching every move she made. On one occasion he followed Beryl and the child through the market and when

Arthur slipped, he picked the child up, patted his head and went his way without speaking to either of them or even smiling at the woman. Everyone found that rather amusing. He always galloped into the town, never cantered, tying the mare to the iron railings surrounding the church. He went into the barber's shop but rarely allowed the barber to cut more than half an inch off his lengthy beard. The barber, who felt he was a lonely man, could never get him to talk about life in the prison. Henderson had also been seen riding across the hills by moorland farmers when moving their flocks into fresh pastures. Always carrying a shotgun with him, the verger had said, possibly because, like the last unfortunate man of the cloth, he was afraid that he might be attacked by prisoners.

Holmes paid him handsomely but it was only when he was about to leave that the verger remembered that the Prison Chaplain had been into the church several times, looking at the list of clergy who had served the church. Something of a historian, the verger reckoned, but that was not the view of my friend.

Lestrade arrived, in a mood more buoyant than I had ever seen him in before. He was, as I had imagined, thankful to be out of the city for a couple of days. Having given all the necessary orders to the constables in Tavistock who knew the area well, and would arrive at ten in the evening, he felt that for his own peace of mind he should take a close look at the terrain. He asked me to walk with him across the moors because he needed to get his bearings before the operation began in earnest. On his previous visit he had only crossed the moor at night in a thick fog, the night on which we had discovered Beryl Stapleton bound and gagged by her husband's hand, in Merripit House, to prevent her from warning Sir Henry of his impending death. On that occasion, Lestrade had remained with the lady in Merripit House while Holmes and I went in search of Stapleton.

There was a slight mist as we ambled through the prehistoric remains of grey stone huts once the homes of the forgotten folk who had lived on the moor. The Inspector was both fascinated by and curious about, two huge monoliths that may have marked their temples.

'On this barren hillside, doctor, what did these people find to live on?'

'They would have kept cattle and would never have been short of sustenance with so much wildlife available; rabbits, foxes, birds.'

'All killed, no doubt, with arrows?'

'Quite likely, arrows tipped with flint.'

'There would be no difficulty hiding away in this terrain, doctor. Not surprising that escaping convicts are able to hold out for so long. A profusion of caves and huts.'

'True, Lestrade, but let's not forget the disused tin mines once used to house the hound we killed two years ago.'

'No, indeed, but tonight, doctor, we are fortunate in knowing the precise location of yet another bestial creature.'

We both stopped short on hearing an unusual bird cry.

'Was that a creature, doctor, or some kind of warning?'

'Could be a curlew, though I am only guessing. I was not reared in these parts, so you must ask the naturalist when you capture him.'

As we were climbing up on to higher ground Lestrade stopped suddenly, asking me to explain the business of the shoe. For a few seconds, I have to admit, I wondered what he was talking about. 'Ah, the shoe, Lestrade!'

He laughed. 'Have you also forgotten? It has been in the back of my mind for several months and time and again I had meant to mention it to Holmes, but it has always slipped my mind. Anno Domini, doctor!'

'Not at all, Inspector. Busy mortals tend to store the trivial in the recesses of their minds. You are alluding to the fact that Holmes mentioned throwing a shoe into Grimpen Mire on the night Stapleton performed his vanishing act.'

'Yes, you have it, doctor. I think at the time you might have mentioned that the pair would have been complete if he hadn't slung it into the mire. What did you mean?'

'History now, Lestrade, but I will enlighten you. Two years ago, Dr Mortimer, who still lives in Grimpen, called at Baker Street to ask my friend's advice. It was Mortimer who examined Sir Charles shortly after his untimely death; a heart attack, as you will remember, caused by the appearance of that ghastly hound. It was he who regaled us with the story of the legend.'

'Are you saying that Mortimer made the journey to London merely to discuss a legend?'

'No. Indeed not. He was in town to welcome Sir Henry, who was about to arrive from Canada, but first he needed

Holmes's advice. He wanted to share the deep feelings of unease he had felt since his discovery that one baronet after another had met a direful end. It was too good an opportunity to miss, so you could say, proverbially, that he killed two birds with a single stone. Dr Mortimer was a realist, a man of science like my friend, a man who had no belief in the supernatural, not until after the death of Sir Charles, when he witnessed such an awesome and horrified expression on the dead man's face.

He brought with him an early eighteenth century manuscript containing a statement on the origin of the legend of the Hound of the Baskervilles by one of Hugo Baskerville's descendents, who described Hugo as a profane and godless man. It appears that one evening, during Michaelmas, Hugo, with five of his ungodly companions, descended on a farm and carried off the farmer's beautiful young daughter. They locked her in an upper chamber while carousing throughout the night. The poor lass must have been terrified by all the singing and shouting going on below and wondering how long it would be before they had their evil way with her. The lass didn't lack courage, she made her escape by climbing down the ivy on the south wall. Once on terra firma she made her way across the moor to her father's farm.

When Hugo found the cage empty, the bird having flown, he rushed downstairs to the dining room, leapt upon the great table, scattering all the flagons and crying out that he would give his soul to the devil if that would aid him in overtaking the wench. The statement says that many of the revellers were aghast, nevertheless the hounds were given the scent of the lass's kerchief and within minutes thirteen men, armed with their pistols at the ready, took horse.'

'No hope for her then?'

'None! Lestrade, take a look at those two great stones at the foot of the hill. There in the bright moonlight the revellers saw the body of the lass, who had either died of fear or fatigue. There too they saw an even grimmer sight, that of a great black beast, shaped like a bloodhound, yet much larger, with blazing eyes and dripping jaws. The creature was tearing out the throat of that profane and wicked baronet. That is where and how the legend originated.

Despite the fact that there were footprints of a giant hound near the body of Sir Charles, the coroner accepted that death was due to a normal and not unexpected heart attack. Mortimer felt that whatever the outcome of the inquest, he was duty bound to produce the historical document regarding the legend for the new baronet to read. It would give Sir Henry a chance to return to Canada if he felt so inclined. Holmes thought in the same vein as Mortimer. The new baronet should be informed.

The following day Sir Henry and Mortimer arrived at Baker Street with a strange tale to tell. Sir Henry, who had spent one night at the Northumberland Hotel in Charing Cross, received a grey envelope containing half a foolscap sheet on which there was a message which read *As you value your life or your reason keep away from the moor.* Sir Henry was angry, saying nothing would keep him away, but how did anyone other than Dr Mortimer know he was staying at the Northumberland? Holmes put his skills into action only to discover that the baronet was being followed everywhere he went. One cabbie was able to describe the man but Holmes rightly surmised that the man who was wearing a beard was in disguise.

The following morning we called at the hotel to see Sir Henry, who was angrily berating a room-steward because one of a new pair of shoes that he had put out to be cleaned was missing. He immediately put an old pair outside the door but only minutes later, there was a repeat performance. Another shoe was missing. Therefore he was left with odd shoes.

Lestrade was quick. 'I know exactly what you are going to tell me, doctor. The used shoe provided the scent for the hound. All that was needed for the murderer to kill his victim without laying hands on him. Not a shot fired, merely another accident. Very clever! Thank God we don't have to deal with many criminals who resort to what you might describe as scientific means.'

As we climbed even higher I was able to point out Merripit House, a bleak moor-land farmhouse once the home of a grazier.

'You recognise the building, do you, Lestrade?'

'I most certainly do, although I last saw it hidden in a thick mist. It's a melancholy place but for Stapleton's machinations, perfect. You are quite sure, are you, doctor, that the animal is always fed and watered around midnight?'

'It is, I can assure you.'

'I wonder where this fellow has his head down?'

'Could be anywhere on the moor, particularly in the direction of Black Tor, where there are hundreds of caves as well as disused mines in a perilous state.'

'Much safer, doctor, for my men to capture him in the act of feeding the animal.'

I smiled inwardly. The local constables had become his men. Excellent!

By ten o'clock the men were all assembled in a field near Grimpen village. Lestrade ordered them to make their way slowly towards the barn. No smoking, no talking. Absolute silence was necessary.

Although there was no moon we were able to fight our way through the bushes without causing a disturbance. Only the sound of a wolf in the distance, the hoot of an owl and nightjars chirping. Twenty minutes later, we were in position. A long long wait, and despite Lestrade's orders, the men were whispering among themselves that this was a wild goose chase. Suddenly the men quietened as we heard the sound of a horse's hooves cantering slowly across the moor. Why so slowly, I had wondered at the time?

As before, the animal began to whimper, followed by ferocious howling as it leapt up, battering itself against the padlocked door. The masked rider leapt off his horse and walked slowly towards the barn door as if feeling his way. As he unlocked the door the dog became even more ferocious and the man, as though afraid, opened the door fractionally before hurling the food into the barn. The howling that had been echoing round the moor, stopped, while the dog audibly chewed its meal. The man picked up the bucket and made his way towards a water butt. After filling the bucket, he entered the barn and had just put the bucket down in front of the dog, when two constables grabbed him. Lestrade gave orders for candles and a hurricane lamp to be lit.

Two of the men, tougher than any one sees in the London Constabulary, hurled the stranger against a wall, telling him he would have no head left and no guts either unless he talked. Lestrade looked the other way. One of the constables was about to remove the mask when the hound leapt up, knocking him to the ground. Far too dangerous to use my pistol because of the close proximity of the men, so I waited a few seconds but was too late. The dog then leapt at the masked man's throat, knocked him to the ground, tore off an ear and his left cheek. Lestrade shot it in the head, killing it instantly. Kneeling beside the man, I removed the blood soaked mask and for several seconds remained frozen.

What had we done? Not Stapleton as expected. I shook my head in disbelief. Lestrade understood the inference and ordered the men to clear out of the barn before kneeling on the man's left side. He held the man's head while I gave him several sips of brandy. With his dying breath James MacDowell, a Scotsman serving a life sentence, gave us his name and despite virtually choking, managed to tell us that he had been given the horse and sufficient funds to reach Dundee by someone called Enders. We later learnt that MacDowell had smothered his mother for the pittance she was going to leave him.

Lestrade told the men to search the barn for a couple of sacks in which the body could be placed before it was strapped across the back of the victim's horse. While they were thus employed, Lestrade took me by the arm. 'Come on,

Doctor, let us take a look at what he was carrying in those bags that are strapped to the horse.'

The two bags told us all we needed to know. In his possession the dead man had a complete change of clothing, a map and a quantity of coins. Somehow the convict, James MacDowell, had been given every possible aid needed to escape from that hell-hole on the moor.

We knew that prisoners serving life were only allowed two visits a year and on those rare visiting days no one, under the watchful eye of the guards, could possibly have given him the clothes. It had to be an inside job. Lestrade and I came to the conclusion that only a prison officer could have been the brains behind the plan to carry out such a near perfect escape. But why was he feeding the animal? Only Holmes would be able to interpret such a bizarre business.

It was two o'clock in the morning before Lestrade and I returned to Baskerville Hall where Holmes, Baskerville, and Beryl Stapleton were waiting for us. I was surprised to see Holmes because he had made a point of not coming face to face with Lestrade in case he embroiled the Inspector in the Mycroft affair.

'Hardly a success story, Holmes,' said Lestrade as we entered the sitting room.

'At least you captured a convict who escaped early yesterday evening.'

Sir Henry and Beryl looked on aghast, while Lestrade stared at me in total disbelief.

He was angry. 'What are you saying, Holmes? Has this exercise been a complete fiasco, and have I been called down from the Yard to deal with a problem that is in Falconby's court?'

'No, Lestrade, quite the contrary. You have proved conclusively that my deductions were correct but, foolishly, I have failed once again to apprehend the man who is one of the most brilliant villains I have met. I would dearly have liked to cross swords with him.'

It was the first time that I had ever heard Holmes castigate himself in such a way. Describing himself as foolish made me realise how much this case meant to him.

'Late yesterday evening, Lestrade, while you and Watson were on the moor I visited the prison, expecting the Chaplain to be absent around midnight because I fully believed he would be making his nightly expedition to feed the creature. On the other hand, if he evaded capture he would return to the prison and I would be there to welcome him while he was still carrying remnants of the food, and the mask in his saddlebag. That was all I needed to prove his guilt. My hypothesis that Stapleton was playing the role of a Chaplain had to be proved. Supposing, Lestrade, that he was on his way to feed the animal when a sixth sense may have alerted him to the fact that Merripit House was surrounded. Even the hound, yowling in an unaccustomed way, may have warned him that the barn was under surveillance. There was only one alternative. A late night call at the prison was the answer.

By ten o'clock I was in a position from which it was possible to observe anyone leaving on horseback. After half an hour's wait I heard a horse cantering towards the open gates. I believed, that at last, my premise would be proved

126

without a doubt, but I realised I was wrong when Falconby, who was on his way home, quite clearly gave the order for the gates to be closed. At that point, despite the late hour, it was essential that I checked whether Henderson was still in his quarters.

Before the guard had time to close the gates I yelled at Falconby to hold fire. Even though I was still in the shadows he recognised my voice, and immediately came to a halt. It was not surprising that he was angry, thinking, no doubt, that I was trying to pull a fast one in an effort to have words with Mycroft. I told him that another matter was equally important and, despite the late hour, I needed to have words with Henderson.

'Impossible, Holmes,' he yelled. 'You must return in the morning.'

'Was the Chaplain,' I asked, 'taking the leave he so richly deserves?'

Falconby snarled at me, no other word for it. 'The Chaplain,' he shouted, 'who is a sick man, is not in a fit enough state to receive visitors at the moment. That is all I have to say on the matter so maybe you'll allow me to return home? I see little enough of my family as it is.'

From that moment there was no turning back. The matter, I told Falconby, was serious but he could quite safely leave it in the hands of a senior officer, because my visit would take no more than ten minutes.

'He's lucky to be alive, Holmes. Five minutes, that's all.'

'I have to say those few words added an urgency to my expedition. In the end Falconby reluctantly dismounted, and took me up to his office. Once there he explained that sometime after dark Henderson had been the victim of an outrageous attack. The felon, who had managed to escape, had not only stolen the little money that Henderson was carrying, but the key to the padlocked stable block was missing, as well as some of Henderson's vestments and his horse. The Chaplain, he said, who was battered and bruised, had been tied up, gagged, and left in one of the stalls. Like the valiant man he is, he had made light of the matter but at that moment he was in sick-bay sleeping it off, hardly the time for a casual visit by someone he had never met. I persisted. Eventually he climbed down and agreed to send one of his officers to the ward to find out whether Henderson would agree to have a few words.

At that moment I began to think that every deduction I had made had been erroneous. Whilst waiting I wandered round the office, gazed at the chessmen and picking up the black king, moved it around the board, wondering what Falconby had been holding back when he first mentioned the black king. I had to start again from scratch, more deductions, logical deductions, in an effort to equate a variety of clues.

The officer returned, saying it would be possible to take a look at Henderson, but he appeared to be in a deep sleep. Falconby, for some reason smiling to himself, told me to feel free to take a look but to be sure to bring flowers for the victim in the morning. He obviously expected me to leave, but suddenly there was a commotion on the floor below. We heard several men shouting then someone ascending the stairs at a rate of knots. An officer, who didn't wait to knock, rushed straight into the room.

Falconby looked aghast at such insubordination, but said nothing. The officer, who hardly took time to draw breath, said that he believed Henderson was dying. Although he was no doctor he thought the pulse was weak, and the prison doctor, who was now at home in Princeton, should be called out. Falconby decided to investigate before taking the matter further. He made no move to invite me to join him but I followed in his wake. It took at least five minutes to reach the ward. Everything was quiet but the guard who should have been keeping an eye on the patients was lying prone on the floor, knocked out with a single blow. Henderson's bed was empty. The blankets were still warm, but the patient had flown the nest. Once again Stapleton had been one step ahead.

'You mean, Mr Holmes, that he had done a runner?' Lestrade looked staggered.

'Yes, but your assistance, Lestrade, in dealing with the second beast, was invaluable in proving that my deductions were correct. Not many hours ago my hypothesis was confirmed when the verger remarked upon the fact that Henderson followed Beryl and the young child round the market, even picked the child up on one occasion, but he never attempted to speak to them, always keeping his head averted. Those brief episodes confirmed my opinion that Stapleton was indeed Henderson, the so-called Chaplain employed on Her Majesty's service at the prison.'

'Damn it, Holmes!' I exclaimed. 'I should have realised that the dying man who kept repeating the word Enders was trying to say Henderson.'

Lestrade was apoplectic. 'Do you mean to tell me that you failed to share these thoughts, or deductions as you call them, with the Doctor?'

'Yes. I am sorry Watson, but I had to be sure, although at several stages I had given you a few clues as to his identity.'

'Which, Holmes, I failed to pick up, so let's not waste any more time. Stapleton must have heard of Lestrade's arrival, put two and two together and sent this wretched convict to feed the animal, take the rap and hope that he would be shot in the process.'

'So where is this villainous man at this moment?' demanded Lestrade.

'I am afraid, Inspector, that I have no idea.'

'You mean he is at liberty?'

At this point Baskerville put his arm round Beryl, who had been crying, and led her from the room.

'He is at liberty, Mr Holmes, because you called at the prison without consulting me. That is fact, is it not?'

'It is, Lestrade, but had I not done so my deductions may never have been proved, so I had better start at the beginning.'

'Not,' said Baskerville as he re-entered the room carrying a whisky decanter and glasses, 'not, my friends, until you have had a drop to restore you.'

'A welcome sight,' said Lestrade, 'and my God I need it.'

'Now, Holmes,' I said, as Sir Henry sat down, 'you can start at the beginning.'

'These are the clues, Watson. You only have to remember that on our return to Paddington two years ago, our journey was considerably delayed because a murder occurred on the train ahead. Neither the victim nor the killer was identified. You agree?'

'Most certainly.'

'A few days ago we visited St Leonard's Church, where we scanned a list of past incumbents. There was only one whose death was not recorded, because he had vanished without trace.'

'Jonathan Williams M.A.'

'Precisely.'

'Oh, my goodness, Holmes, how blind I have been.'

Lestrade looked astonished. 'This is the first time I have heard anything about a murder on the Paddington Express.'

'Nowhere near your area, Inspector. This murder took place shortly after the train left Exeter. All my deductions have been proved. Now you have the answer, Watson.'

'The victim,' I said, 'was the Reverend Jonathan Williams, murdered by Stapleton, who stole all his clothes, adopted the role of a man of the cloth and changed his appearance.'

'The story Falconby told us at lunch,' said Baskerville slowly, 'about meeting a man of the cloth was false.'

'No, that was true, but the tale Stapleton told him about a wife who died giving birth in the north was a fabrication.'

Baskerville was angry. 'He should never have taken the man on board without a reference.'

'There may have been a reason for that strategy. A development we must investigate later.'

Baskerville rose, and walking up and down the room kept muttering to himself until, at last, he asked Holmes what he was going to do now he knew for sure that Stapleton had assumed the role of Henderson and had not been sucked into Grimpen Mire.

Holmes looking at Lestrade said, 'It depends on the Inspector.'

Lestrade looked puzzled. 'What are you saying? Holmes?'

'There is one way to ensure the safety of these three precious people. A diversion is the answer. First of all, Sir Henry, let the staff know that you are contemplating a long holiday. Mention that you will be leaving for Brighton tomorrow with Mrs Stapleton and the child, not forgetting to mention that Doctor Watson will be accompanying you.'

Baskerville sat down, shaking his head, but with a broad smile on his face. He was like a child entering into the spirit of a new adventure.

'Make sure you catch the 10 a.m. train to Paddington but do not arrive at the station in Tavistock until the last minute.'

At that point I interrupted, to make it crystal clear that I would be with them all the way. Baskerville clapped his hands.

'You will not go to Brighton,' continued Holmes, 'nor change trains at Reading because you will be staying in London, not at one of the well-known central hotels, but one in a quiet area near Hampstead Heath.'

'No need for that, Holmes,' I said breaking his train of thought. 'Mary and I will be only too pleased to entertain guests.'

'Watson, that is precisely what I hoped you would suggest. When you reach Paddington take a hansom direct to the Northumberland Hotel, have the luggage unloaded and enter the hotel. Once inside, tell the doorman that you have made a mistake and that you should have been taken to the Ritz. Sit in the foyer for ten minutes, then take another cab and make your way back to Watson's residence in Paddington.'

'Excellent, Holmes,' said Lestrade, 'quite excellent. Now, Sir Henry, I will be able to return your generous hospitality by having Doctor Watson's house and surgery kept under surveillance. You will be as safe there as anywhere in the country.'

'Thank you, gentlemen,' said an emotional man with tears in his eyes. Beryl will be relieved. I will let her know at once, packing will give her something to occupy her mind.'

All I can say is that it was one of the most satisfactory stratagems that Holmes had ever devised. A few hours later, despite the fact that Holmes thought that he and the Inspector should travel on different trains, they caught the Paddington Express.

Lestrade shrugged off the matter, saying he would fight his corner if and when!

CHAPTER TWELVE

Once back home in Baker Street, Holmes lost no time in organising a unit of irregulars, with twelve-year old Billy in command. They were given orders that on the morrow they were to track doormen or porters leaving the Home Office, make a note of their names and addresses, then return with all speed to Baker Street, where they would be given further instructions.

In the early hours of the following morning Holmes was presented with the names and addresses of three of the men but Billy, dejected and crestfallen, admitted that he had been unsuccessful. It was fortuitous that he had heard an official telling Taylor to get moving and not hang about. Taylor, the man whom he had followed and never let out of his sight, made straight for the *Red Dragon* in Victoria Street, carrying a rough old bag. He entered the public house just as Big Ben struck seven. During the next five hours Billy, on several occasions, tried creeping into the bar but was unceremoniously thrown out by the publican. At midnight, when the pub closed, Taylor had failed to materialise and Billy thought he had failed.

Holmes congratulated him on providing most interesting evidence. It was an excellent piece of detection that could possibly prove to be most valuable to the course of the investigation.

After handing them each a shilling for work well done, usually my job, I hasten to add, Holmes gave them their orders for the following day. Much more difficult to achieve this time.

They were told to loiter about in the vicinity of the Home Office. If anyone emerged from the building needing a cab, they were to listen closely to the address the cabbie was given. They must then make tracks to the address in order to discover the name of the official. In all cases it was important to remember what the man looked like. Holmes knew ordinary clerks could not afford to hire cabs but what he desperately needed to do was trace at least one man who had worked closely with his brother. One man who could be trusted to provide him with sufficient evidence enabling him to trace the devil who was pointing the finger at Mycroft.

During the day, while the street Arabs were tracking officials, Holmes paid a visit to the *Red Dragon*. Wearing a disreputable old cloak and battered hat, he sat in a corner, shades of the old man in Tavistock, keeping an eye on the comings and goings of hardened drinkers. After three hours he was rewarded for his patience when a smartly dressed man in a tweed suit, obviously manufactured in Germany, entered the bar.

Before ordering the man glanced swiftly round the saloon, hardly bothering with the down-at-heel individual hidden behind a haze of smoke. Holmes, whose hearing is acute, heard him ask for a double dram of Hock. Such an odd request immediately alerted my friend. The surly publican, nodding at the man, opened a door, allowing the stranger access to his living quarters. The phrase *Double dram of Hock* was obviously used as a password.

Holmes then knew, to his satisfaction, why Billy had been left outside the premises for five hours, killing time. Taylor, as we later discovered, had entered the *Red Dragon* at the front of the building but made his exit at the rear. Holmes, who had been about to inspect the rear of the building, sat down again when a well-dressed middle-aged man entered. The man, obviously English, well-built of swarthy complexion, wearing spectacles and carrying an attaché case, nodded at the publican as the door to the living quarters was once again thrown open.

Holmes slouched out of the *Red Dragon*, made his way across the road, and standing in the shadows of a mulberry tree, could clearly observe both the front and the back of the building. Within an hour both men re-appeared. The foreigner in the tweed suit, who was now carrying the attaché case, turned left and the Englishman turned right into Victoria Street. Holmes was faced with a dilemma. He needed to know what was in the attaché case, but the place of origin of the material was of equal importance, resulting in his decision to follow the Englishman down Victoria Street.

His quarry, who was in no hurry, walked with the ease of a man well pleased with himself, a man who had just completed a difficult assignment. At the end of Victoria Street the man, totally unaware that he was being stalked, crossed Parliament Square then left into Whitehall as he made his way towards Trafalgar Square. Suddenly he stopped to speak to a woman who was running towards the entrance to the Home Office. For some minutes they appeared to be arguing before becoming reconciled. He then pecked her on the cheek before entering the Home Office, where the doorman saluted him.

The woman, some thirty years old, with blonde hair, pale blue eyes and dressed in a expensive dark green outfit, turned suddenly, coming face to face with Holmes, whom she scarcely noticed because she was intent on hailing a cab. Holmes, much to his annoyance, was unable to hear the directions given to the cabbie and watched helplessly as the cab turned on its axis and sped down Whitehall towards Westminster Abbey.

During the afternoon Holmes called at a house in the most squalid area of Vauxhall, where one of the doormen lodged. Nothing more than a hovel, he had said, hardly the place one would expect to find an undercover agent. He also visited two houses in Lambeth, one in a grubby back street, where Holmes spoke to the man's mother, who was a permanent invalid suffering from tuberculosis. He kept his distance, but was genuinely moved by the love and care she was receiving from her son and daughter-in-law. They never left her on her own at night nor over the weekend. Holmes decided that such a man would not have had the time to be involved in any sort of undercover work.

At the next house, in a more prepossessing street, he met Mrs Evans, two of her four children and her parents. All three generations living quite happily in a small house in which, so Holmes said, there was hardly room to swing a cat. Two rooms upstairs, two rooms downstairs and facilities in the backyard, where there was a fair show of pot plants. The walls in the house were covered with holy pictures, crucifixes and pictures of the Queen, leading Holmes to believe that Evans, a confirmed royalist, might well be persuaded to act as an inside man and play his part in saving the monarchy from ignominious scandals. We knew, from experience, that porters who spend much of their time standing around pick up a great deal of information by doing nothing more than keeping their eyes and ears open. Really a question of what the butler saw. All Holmes had to work with was Hugh Evans and possibly Taylor, the man whom Billy had followed.

Mrs Evans told Holmes that her husband was a stickler for time. He finished his duty at six o'clock, and by the time Big Ben struck the quarter he was at the north end of Lambeth Bridge. He always turned left on to the bridge, never deviating because his two older children often went to meet him. Holmes, having looked at a wedding photograph and another of Evans as a young man in army uniform, asked Mrs Evans whether she would object if he met her husband on the bridge. She looked a bit taken aback, but relaxed the moment Holmes explained that he was carrying out an enquiry into the way the lower echelons in the government service were treated. You are right to do so, she had told him. 'The men only have a few days off a year while the bosses take weeks, even months, in some cases.'

Holmes would have recognised Evans without ever having seen a photograph. He saw a tired man, no more than five foot three or four inches, walking with a slight limp across the bridge whilst keeping an eye out for his children. Evans was quite startled when Holmes addressed him. After a few minutes conversation, during which time Holmes explained that he had the future of the monarchy at heart, Evans agreed to talk further, so the two men made their way to a bench alongside the river, with Lambeth Palace towering behind them. Evans was astonished to learn that he was talking to the most famous consulting detective in the land, a man whose brother was languishing in a convicts' prison. It is not possible, Evans had maintained, that Mr Mycroft Holmes could have committed treason. He was such an honest man, who worked harder than anyone else in the building and took fewer holidays. Not only that, he made sure that all the lackeys working in his department received a generous Christmas box.

At long last, after gaining a clear picture of the internal workings of Mycroft's office, Holmes posed a question about two words that had been troubling him. Two words Mycroft had uttered as he and Watson had left Falconby's office.

He asked Evans if he had heard any murmurs about the Steiffel Affair.

The doorman laughed until tears ran down his cheek. 'That was the word,' he choked, 'that us lowly drudges had used. Stifle is summat to be kept quiet, summat hidden.'

'Ah!' said Holmes. 'Stifle not Steiffel! Tell me more.'

'Well it's like this, sir. Everyone in the building knew that when Colonel Falconby was working in the Home Office he had been short of the ready. Gambling, living the high life and all that, which is why he took on Sid Laurel, a well-known ringer, as head groom.'

It appears that Laurel, on Falconby's behalf, had acquired two horses, a speedy animal and one of medium pace. The ringer painted Zeus, the fast horse, to look like Adamant, the medium pacer, then entered it at Newmarket, but the laugh was on the Colonel in more ways than one, because the Horseguards were called out to deal with a riot, which meant he missed the chance to see his horse win. Adamant, the horse on which he had laid a £200 wager at fifteen to one, won by two lengths but as it cantered back to the enclosure to the plaudits of the crowd, the heavens opened. Not just a sprinkling of rain, but an enormous deluge, an act of God that washed off much of the paint on Adamant, leading, as one would expect, to a stewards' enquiry. Falconby denied all knowledge of the scam but Sid Laurel, who had escaped justice many times for similar offences, was given twelve months. Three months later, when Falconby's father died, he inherited the title and an estate including a large manor house in Devon. We learnt later that Falconby was permanently scarred by the Stifle Affair. His name was never put forward for high ranking government posts, and when he was offered the job at Princeton, his wife, who hated all the scandal attached to their name, persuaded him to move down to his seat in Devon for good.'

For me, having had the word stifle interpreted would have been sufficient to explain Mycroft's outburst, but not for Holmes, who believed there was much more at stake. He asked Hugh Evans if he would keep an eye on Taylor, who might be involved in nefarious activities detrimental to the state.

Evans, who enjoyed verbal jokes, as the stifle affair had demonstrated, told my friend that Sniffy Taylor wouldn't harm a fly, but he was everybody's dogsbody. Sniffy will run here, run there, do anyone's bidding. Taylor, apparently, had been nicknamed by the underlings as Sniffy because he was a continual sniffer whose sufferings were exacerbated when cleaners raised clouds of dust. His wife had left him, he drank too much and often arrived in the morning worse for wear, but Evans was positive that he would never be involved in a plot to sabotage the country.

Holmes recognised that it was a long shot but he wanted to know what was in the rough old bag Taylor had been carrying, for whom it was intended, and who was the mastermind behind his visit to the *Red Dragon*. He was about to ask Evans to act as his inside man when the sound of children running towards the bench caught him in mid sentence. Evans lifted his daughter onto his lap while the boy ran round and round the bench. 'We won't talk any more, Holmes had whispered to Evans, 'but come to 221B Baker Street tonight.'

Following Holmes's directions to the letter, Sir Henry made it known to the staff that he would be taking a long holiday with Dr Watson, Mrs Stapleton and Arthur.

Palmer drove us to Tavistock, where we arrived only five minutes before the train was due to leave. Thinking young Arthur might be a problem, Baskerville had reserved a compartment, which meant that with four spare seats we were able to stretch our limbs. The child, naturally excited at experiencing the first train journey of his life, was engrossed asking interminable questions about the herds of animals in the fields, and why so many churches and houses. His formative years had been spent isolated in the country, with occasional visits to the market in Tavistock, but many of the questions amused us and enlivened the journey.

As soon as Sir Henry closed his eyes I slipped out of the compartment and made my way along the corridor to take a close look at all the passengers. Several people glanced in my direction but no one, I am quite sure, had ever seen me before. Stapleton had, of course, seen me on the moor and had he been on the train keeping track of his wife and child, his eyes would surely have given him away.

On our arrival at Paddington a porter, carrying our cases on his head, led the way to the line of waiting cabs. Once the luggage was loaded and all were on board, I asked the cabbie, in a loud voice, to make for the Northumberland Hotel. All this, of course, within earshot of the porter. Shortly after we left Paddington, Baskerville began to look distinctly uneasy. Beryl, oblivious to the fact, continued answering the child's questions and pointing out the landmarks. As we drove across Hyde Park Sir Henry grasped my arm.

'There's a fellow on horseback, Doctor, who has been following us all the way.' Probably owing to the fact that I was listening to the chat between mother and son I had been totally unaware of any danger. Turning to take a good look, I breathed a sigh of relief when I recognised the constable who, on Lestrade's orders, had arrested Lady Loubes-Bernac. Baskerville relaxed once again but not for long. I shouted to the wizened old man driving the hansom to make a diversion past Buckingham Palace, down Constitutional Hill and into Parliament Square before driving up Whitehall.

He laughed, 'Want to see the sights, do you Guv?'

'Yes please,' shouted Arthur and Beryl in unison.

After we clambered out of the vehicle, the luggage, as Holmes had suggested, was taken into the Northumberland Hotel. I then went to reception to ask for the keys to our rooms. Nothing, of course, had been reserved, so I apologised, said we should have been taken to the Ritz. Ten minutes later we left the hotel, as directed, and made our way to my place in Paddington where Mary, bless her, welcomed her guests, and as usual had them feeling at home only minutes after they had crossed the threshold.

After dinner I made my way to Baker Street, arriving at 8 o'clock, shortly before Hugh Evans.

There was something quite likeable about the chap. He overcame his smallness of stature by his demeanour, by the way he entered the room, and by the way he stood looking one straight in the face with those intelligent, hazel eyes.

Holmes, I knew, had expected to get through the matter in hand in twenty minutes, his normal procedure, but we enjoyed the exchanges so much that Evans was with us for well over an hour.

Hugh Evans and I had more than a little in common. We were both army men. He had joined the Welsh Fusiliers when he was a lad of fifteen. It was a life he enjoyed, seeing the world at the Queen's expense, much more instructive than being incarcerated in the bowels of a Welsh mine in the Rhonda Valley. When he was stationed in London he met and married Annie, who proved to be a sensible lass. Knowing her husband could be called to fight anywhere in the world at a moment's notice, she decided to remain in her parents' house. She made the right decision because a few months after their marriage, his wife already pregnant, Evans was posted to South Africa where he fought in the First Boer War in 1880-81. By this time he was serving as a batman to Major Honfleur, a man he admired and to whom he became very attached. Evans was injured in 1881, shrapnel in the upper leg, but thanks to the Major he was invalided out of the army and given a permanent job at the Home Office.

Unusual for Holmes, I must say, but he encouraged Evans to talk about his background, about his father who had been a Wesleyan pastor in a Welsh tabernacle and who had died when his son was fifteen, leaving the family destitute. Nothing for it but to enlist in the army. The fact that his father had been a pastor explained why Evans was well-read, intelligent and communicative.

As Holmes said later, Hugh Evans was probably more intelligent than half the clerks in the Home Office, but the state of affairs fitted the plans Holmes had in mind. First of all he needed a list of all the government officers who had worked closely with Mycroft, their hobbies, their clubs, political leanings and their addresses.

Interrupting, I said, in a nonchalant manner, 'The Hanover Club sounds interesting.'

'It must be, sir, because more and more of them are joining.'

'Do they need to be sponsored?' asked Holmes.

'I wouldn't think so. It all happens too quickly for them to be elected, not like the Athenaeum, the Garrick or the Diogenes, where they have to wait for months.'

'Have you any idea,' I asked, 'why it is called the Hanover?'

'I guess it's because it happens to be in Hanover Square. Sniffy had to deliver a box of papers to the club, for Mr Gregory it was, and he couldn't believe his eyes when he went into the place. Every wall is covered with pictures of

18th and 19th century kings and queens. All the Georges, and Williams and our good queen.'

'He's a historian is he, this Sniffy?' enquired Holmes with a broad grin.

'Doesn't have to be, sir, the names were all written underneath.'

'So why does Sniffy get these jobs, Mr Evans?'

'Not sure, Doctor, but he likes them 'cos they always give him a drink or even two. Don't think he's supposed to talk but when he's had a few, well you know what happens, he spills the beans.'

Holmes, his eyes glittering in expectation, said that he would like to share those beans, particularly relating to one evening quite recently, when Sniffy, carrying an old canvas bag, had called at the *Red Dragon*, entered the inner sanctum, then failed to reappear.

Evans, said that Sniffy always carried out orders to the letter, which meant that he would have been told to enter the living quarters, hand over papers, or whatever he was carrying, to a third party, then make himself scarce.

It was at this point during the evening that Holmes asked Evans if he would be prepared to act as an inside man, keeping him informed of any dubious activity, particularly with reference to anyone who was a member of the Hanover Club.

Evans, only too eager to oblige, made it clear that it would make his job infinitely more interesting. As Holmes reached for his wallet, Evans said that he could not accept payment, what he was doing was for his country. Holmes, touched at the man's loyalty, insisted on giving him ten guineas to spend on his children's needs.

I watched Evans striding jauntily down Baker Street, his limp barely noticeable, his head held high. There, I told myself, went yet another man with a mission.

CHAPTER THIRTEEN

For the next few days I took up residence again in Baker Street, leaving Mary more room to accommodate our guests. It also meant that I was on hand if anything untoward occurred.

When I rose the following morning I found Holmes, who had been up since five, still in his dressing-gown, browsing through history books. A rare occurrence! In fact I had never seen him so engrossed in a subject unrelated to science. Picking up one of the books covering the Hanoverian succession from the end of Queen Anne's reign to the ascent of Queen Victoria, I asked him what he hoped to achieve.

'All I am doing, Watson, is reading what Professor Moriarty must have been studying for the past year or two, maybe more. I believe that he has insinuated himself into the heart of a monumental plot, not of his own making, but one which serves his purpose. One in which so many wheels have been set in motion that it will be difficult to unhinge even one of them. It is an intricate web of massive proportions. Every move he has made has had only one objective and that is to unseat me, although the distinguished personage who now values his advice and who is masterminding the entire operation, is totally unaware of the fact.'

'Are you trying to prove, Holmes, that the arrest of Mycroft is directly related to Moriarty's desire to see you ousted as the most successful consulting detective in Europe?'

'Yes. Precisely that!'

I have to say, at the time, I thought my friend had gone too far. 'Holmes you must be more explicit. How can the Hanoverian Succession be remotely linked to your premeditated downfall?'

'It has everything to do with Moriarty's evil stratagems. Carefully planned, and difficult to unravel, but unravel it I will. However, we have something more immediate to deal with. I know that we both feel very strongly that the wretched clergyman who was murdered on the train and buried in a pauper's grave must be exhumed, and given a decent burial followed by a memorial service in St Leonard's Church.'

'Indeed he must.'

'I will write to the Reverend and Mrs Pyke, asking them to call on his widow who will have been grieving for two years but may find some peace once she knows where her husband is buried. So many sleepless nights, never giving up, always praying that he would return.'

During breakfast, while Holmes was engaged in writing to the Pykes and showing little interest in consuming the excellent fare Mrs Hudson had produced, I had a sudden flash of memory, not déjà vu, but something that actually happened. I was back in the Diogenes, my one and only brief visit to the club, where an unpleasant fellow had called me a spy. Then it hit me!

The Englishman Holmes had seen entering the *Red Dragon*, was a well-dressed, middle-aged man of swarthy complexion, wearing spectacles, but had he, I wondered, flecked green eyes? In polite society he would have asked me to withdraw, not shouted and gesticulated in such a vitriolic manner. More than anything else, it was the sheer and utter hatred in his eyes that shook me at the time.

Holmes suddenly looked up. 'You have not moved a muscle for many minutes, Watson, so tell me, what thoughts of great magnitude have crossed your mind?'

'I was wondering whether the member of the Diogenes who called me a spy could have been the man who tailed Mycroft on the fatal night he returned to the Home Office? Maybe he was the man you saw in the *Red Dragon*, the man who made tracks for the Home Office?'

'The unknown man,' murmured Holmes, after I had shared my misgivings. 'Could well be, Watson, although I could not see the colour of his eyes nor yet the flecks! However, it's imperative that you return to the club, get the fellow's name and find out where he resides.'

I was amazed. 'You don't really think that I will be allowed into such hallowed quarters ever again, Holmes?'

'Watson, you must strike while the iron's hot. Visit the club at once while the cleaners are still at work. Ask to see the secretary, make the excuse that are you are seeking membership. It's a hundred to one chance that there will be a doorman on duty, bored with his day-to-day ritual, and only too willing to talk.'

Holmes was right. Saunders, the man on duty, who had all the attributes needed by a wrestler, was only too willing to talk. A break from his monotonous chores. He told me that there was a waiting list so long that would-be members often waited for two years, but on the other hand, if your face fits! Need I say more? I then asked if Mr Mycroft Holmes was a full member of the club.

'Full member, sir! He was a founder member and it's not right that he's been black-balled.'

'Black-balled! Supposing, Saunders, that he's not guilty. What then?'

'More than half the members, sir, believe that Mr Mycroft is innocent but nobody can answer the questions raised by Mr Charles Boyce, who was once his closest friend.'

Knowing Mycroft, I doubt if he had any close friends. 'Boyce, you say?'

'Yes. He worked closely with Mr Mycroft at the Home Office. It was Boyce who made it quite clear to members that he knew which papers had been destroyed and who was responsible for sending the leaflets inciting people to rebel and demonstrate against the monarchy.'

'Tell me, Saunders,' I asked quickly, 'what colour are Boyce's eyes?'

He frowned as he tried to picture the man. 'Difficult to say, sir. He wears specs but they could be something between green and hazel, sort of dotted you know.'

'Green flecks?'

'Yes, sir, green flecks!'

'And what do you think, Saunders, about Boyce's ideas?'

'I no longer believe a word the geezer says. The story gets hotter by the minute. He's forever talking about spies and every time members get together in the Strangers' Room he opens his big mouth.'

Oh yes! I had a perfect picture in my mind of the man who had accused me of being a spy.

'He's not the only one who gases on about spies. His shadow does the same?'

'Shadow?'

'That Mr Macey who works with 'im. Can't mistake 'im. Swarthy-faced, well-built guy. Can't ever be polite. Looks like a tramp.'

'Does Boyce belong to any other club?'

'Not one of any importance, sir, except for that new one that started up a few months ago. A drinking den, that's all it is.'

'You mean the Hanover?'

'Aye, the Hanover. He paused for a moment with a puzzled expression on his face. 'If you're thinking of joining this club, sir, you should come back and see the secretary, but you're not really their kind.'

'What are you saying, Saunders?'

'Well, sir, you're more friendly, more willing to talk to the likes of me, than the fellows who join this club. You're more like a doctor than a lawyer or a business man, if you don't mind me saying so.'

I laughed. 'You must have studied human nature.'

'I have a lot of time on my hands, sir, nothing else to do, see all sorts here.'

'You are most astute, Saunders. I am a doctor.'

He looked at me open-mouthed, then laughed. 'Astute! That's what my wife's always saying, but that's not quite the word she uses. She says I'm a nosey parker, that's why nothing gets past me.'

'And did you not find Mr Mycroft friendly?'

'Oh, don't get me wrong. He was always polite, he could smile, but he never talked. He was a good gentleman and even if he gets hanged I'll never believe he harmed the country or the Queen, but if it had been Mr........'

He stopped short. I knew exactly what he was going to say.

'So,' said Holmes, when I returned to Baker Street, 'Charles Boyce, who worked closely with Mycroft is the catalyst, and Macey, you say, is his shadow. There will be others in the ring but we must now investigate the Hanover. This lunchtime you must visit the club, show an interest in joining, and ask to see a list of the members.'

'If Boyce is there he will recognise me and accuse me, once again, of spying.'

'Nonsense, Watson! He'll take his meals in the Home Office restaurant, making sure he hears every whisper of day-to-day business.'

'I am sorry, Holmes, but today is not convenient because Mary is expecting me.'

'A couple of hours, Watson?'

I then had a brilliant idea, or so I thought! 'Holmes, why not go yourself in the disguise of Dr Breucot?'

'Because, Watson, in two days time I shall be playing the role in Dresden. Now I have to make haste to catch the boat-train to Harwich.'

'Boat-train!' I was thunderstruck. 'What is going on, Holmes?'

'Not a lot of time, my friend, for fulsome explanations, but I intend to be present in two days time at a gala performance of *The Flying Dutchman* at the *Sächsische Staatoper* in Dresden, the scene of its first performance.'

I was speechless.

'A pity,' he said shaking his head, 'that Richard Wagner is with us no more. To have seen him conducting his own work would have made everything else worthwhile. However, after the performance, if fortune favours the brave --- no, no, it has nothing whatever to do with fortune – success depends solely on deduction and impeccable planning.'

'Success in doing what?' I asked angrily.

'You have a right to be angry, but you have to be here, Watson, because I am depending on you to hold the fort in my absence.'

'Holmes, it's obvious that matters here can't be left to chance. We have to deal with Stapleton immediately, otherwise Baskerville will be at risk when he returns to the Hall. His days will be numbered. At the same time, should we not be concentrating on proving that Mycroft is innocent of all charges?'

'For the moment, Watson, we have nothing to fear from Stapleton because I believe his wings are clipped, not permanently, but long enough to give us room to manoeuvre. As for proving my brother's innocence, we can do no more in this country until we have the measure of Charles Boyce and his associates abroad. Get hold of Evans and ask him to keep an eye on Boyce and contact young Billy, who has an antennae sharper than any policeman.'

Had you noticed, Holmes, that Billy now has two missing incisors?

'Ah, fisticuffs, no doubt! He's a determined lad, but tell him no brawls on my account. Make sure he keeps a watch on the *Red Dragon*. We need to know whether Sniffy Taylor makes regular deliveries and who the fellow is who wears a tweed suit and a bizarre, but unforgettable, tweed hat. If the wearer sporting this hat puts in an appearance, tell Billy to follow him and find out in which hotel he is staying. The man's a foreigner, he may not be here long. A name would be an invaluable asset.'

While I cooled my heels this side of the water Holmes made his way to Harwich to board the Hamburg ferry. A journey, providing the sea was calm, that normally took no more that 24 hours.

Before contacting Billy to give him his orders, I returned to Paddington to make sure that Mary was quite content looking after her guests. She was joyously happy. Most of all she had enjoyed taking Arthur to see the changing of the guard at Buckingham Palace, followed by a visit to the zoo in Regent's Park. While she was acting as cicerone, Sir Henry and Beryl Stapleton, having been left to their own devices, enjoyed a few hours in the National Gallery before walking down to the Thames to gaze at the river traffic.

Mary, always long suffering, was quite disappointed when I explained that because the case was so important I had to return to Baker Street. She said that she fully realised its importance because there were many more policemen on the beat and no matter where they went there was always at least one policeman in the vicinity. Knowing that Lestrade, a man of his word, was protecting our visitors, I returned to Baker Street in a calmer frame of mind.

At seven o'clock that evening, whilst I was eating fish pie, Mrs Hudson's speciality, I heard three, short sharp knocks at the front door. Knowing it was Evans, I shouted to Mrs Hudson to let him come straight up.

He entered the room glowing, the only expression I can use to describe his countenance. I told him to sit down, relax, and enjoy a beer before we got down to business, but bursting with the success of what he had achieved, he could not wait, not even five minutes. He handed me a list of four names, all men who had worked closely with Mycroft. Not only had Evans provided their names and addresses, but he had added a more than adequate biography of each man. He had been able to accomplish this feat because he had volunteered to take over the night duty of a sick colleague. An opportunity which gave him access to the offices of the four men who had liaised with Mycroft over matters relating to both Home and Foreign Office finances. Only two of the men, Charles Boyce and Geoffrey Featherstone, were members of the Hanover. The other two men were coming up to retirement age at the end of the year and it seemed unlikely that they would jeopardise a comfortable existence by being involved in an anti-monarchist plot.

To arrive at this conclusion, I had tried to think as Holmes would have thought. One of the men, a Nicholas Williams, had eleven grandchildren and the other, MacDonald, spent every leave at his hunting lodge in Scotland. With such a large family I could not imagine Williams taking any risks, and I am quite sure that no Scot would ever give up his hunting, shooting and fishing to depose a Queen who loved his country.

Charles Boyce, whom Holmes had described as the catalyst, lived in West Halkin Street in the West End and, according to the notes Evans had scribbled down, he made constant business trips to Amsterdam, even on occasions taking his wife Erica. In fact, he had left that afternoon, and was not expected back for two days.

Geoffrey Featherstone, for whom work took second place, was writing a history of the British monarchy from the fall of Harold to the present day. His visits to the Hanover always took place in the early evening, possibly because he lived in Hampstead and saw no sense in making the journey into the West End twice in one day.

After perusing the notes for a second time I thanked Evans for his assistance, but he had not finished. He had a great deal more to impart. I have to say that I was uneasy about a family man risking his regular job by becoming embroiled in unravelling the truth about a highly inflammable plot to depose the queen. However, he was an intelligent man and must have weighed the odds. Evans related how after Sniffy Taylor had downed a few he asked him, jokingly, whether he carried the crown jewels to a public house in Victoria Street. Sniffy had laughed, saying it was like the game of pass the parcel. He was given a large sealed envelope that he put in his bag, and when it was delivered with the seal unbroken, the landlord rewarded him with a pint. Evans did not believe for one moment that Sniffy would have lived to tell the tale had the seal been broken. On one occasion Sniffy had said that there was a man waiting for him, a foreigner dressed in a tweed suit who gave him half a guinea, then told him to beat it. This was the man Billy had been instructed to follow.

Holmes would have applauded Evans for his devotion to the cause but what he really needed to know was what the envelope contained. Too late now, but I knew my friend would find a way round the impasse.

Again I congratulated Evans on his perspicacity and thanked him for his invaluable assistance. 'No need, sir,' he had said, 'because the last few days have been the most interesting I have experienced since being invalided out of the army.'

As he picked up his hat I said we had better call a cab but he declined, saying it would be safer not to be seen leaving Baker Street. He would catch a tramcar in Marylebone Road that would drop him on the south side of Lambeth Bridge.

After Evans left I realised there was no time like the present — grasp the nettle and get moving. With Boyce away for two days, an evening visit to the Hanover would be more profitable than calling at midday. Members, hopefully in their cups, would be more relaxed, more likely to be discussing politics and the present unrest in the country. Holmes, I knew, would approve my strategy.

It was 9.30 before I set foot in the club. An attendant, making no attempt to check my identity or membership, took my hat and cloak. I made straight for the bar and ordered a brandy. The place sounded like the debating society at my old school, everyone talking and no one listening. All the chaps were wanting to pitch in and at times it was impossible to hear precisely what was being discussed. There was only one way to achieve my objective. I ordered a second brandy and as one of the fellows made a move to leave, I slipped smartly into his chair. No one challenged me because they were engrossed in discussing rumours that had been circulating for some time about the Kaiser wanting to rid himself of the Iron Chancellor, all of which had been reported in the British Press.

One chap described Bismark as a Pomeranian Pirate who'd lost his way. Another angrily disagreed with the sentiment, maintaining that the unification of the German states had been masterminded by a brilliant politician. The rumours, it struck me, could have some truth, for Wilhelm II, who had become Kaiser on the death of his father, apparently wanted to direct both Home and Foreign affairs himself. 'For the Kaiser's dreams,' said a man standing at the bar, 'Bismark was too old and in his dotage.' A nodding of head and general agreement, but what surprised me most was a remark that Bismark would never have approved expansion dependent on yet another war. 'Expansion without pain is the answer,' said one tall, redheaded chap who was standing at the back of the room, 'and in the present circumstances easily achieved.'

At the time, although I had no idea what the fellow was talking about, I found the conversation intriguing and was quite annoyed when the debate was interrupted by a steward rushing in to announce that there had been another

158

demonstration in Whitehall. There was a short discussion as to tactics before two fellows volunteered to take a look at what was happening and report back. It was obvious to me that the majority of the men had no desire to be embroiled. For some reason they had to keep their heads down. Nevertheless, they needed to know precisely what was going on. At this point I decided to make myself scarce. Waiting until another discussion was in full swing, I crept out and made my way back to Baker Street.

Stepping out of the hansom, I caught a glimpse of a small figure squatting on the doorstep, all huddled up, his arms wrapped tightly round his legs for warmth.

'You got a beggar there!' roared the cabbie. 'Don't expect to see them sort in this part of town.'

'Better on my doorstep than in a gutter in the East End,' I retorted sharply. He had no answer and after I had paid him he made off at speed without even a thank you.

Billy stood up grinning sheepishly. 'Didn't take me long to track the geezer, but as Mr Holmes aint in I thought I had better wait for you.'

As I unlocked the door and stepped inside, Mrs Hudson, who was not her usual placid self, appeared. She looked at Billy and told me that he had called two hours ago and that he could have sat in the hall, had he explained himself. I asked her to make the lad a hot drink while I took him upstairs.

Billy's surveillance proved that Holmes had made the right deduction. The man in the tweed coat and curious hat was a foreigner, a certain Herr Ernbach, who was staying at the *Regent Hotel* in Victoria Street, only a stone's throw from the

Red Dragon. The only information Billy was unable to obtain was how long the German was staying in this country.

As soon as he had imbibed a hot cup of cocoa I gave him a shilling, and sent him on his way.

After recording the day's events I quaffed a stiff nightcap before retiring. Lying in bed, I fell asleep wondering exactly what the fellows at the Hanover were planning. It was almost as though they were trying to prove a point, one that many of them were finding hard to accept.

CHAPTER FOURTEEN

Holmes, after his Dresden venture, returned to Baker Street looking tired but not too weary to relate the events of the past few days. The ferry, he said, had arrived in Hamburg at the designated time to link with the Hamburg to Dresden express. Having already telegraphed from London before he left to reserve a single compartment on the express, and knowing the German expertise in travel arrangements, he was not surprised, on arrival, to be shown directly to a reasonably comfortable sleeping berth. The train stopped at both Hanover and Leipzig but he waited until it had pulled out of Leipzig before, once again, assuming the role of Dr Breucot. Arriving in Dresden, he emerged from the train as a distinguished Austrian doctor more concerned with the mind than with the body.

Dr Breucot had also telegraphed the *Residenzschloss* to reserve an apartment for two days. The reason for staying in such luxurious surroundings was that it gave him prestige among the people he hoped to be meeting during the next two days. Holmes was most impressed with the *Residenzschloss,* a magnificent structure built between the 15th and 17th centuries, and once the former residence of the Wettin family. He also enjoyed wandering through an extra extension completed only months before.

Knowing the performance of *The Flying Dutchman* would be fully subscribed, Holmes enlisted the help of Herr Mahler, the director of the *Residenzschloss* whom he, quite rightly, assumed would know how to obtain a late cancellation. Logic paid off, for within two hours he was presented with a ticket for a seat in the stalls.

My friend lost no time finding his bearings in this magnificent city. The *Sächsische Staatoper* and the *Zwinger*, the most famous building in Dresden, were both within walking distance of his hotel. He planned, and succeeded, in gate-crashing a reception for Kaiser Wilhelm II and his wife, Augusta, that took place in the *Wallpavilion*, one of the many pavilions in the *Zwinger*. Heavily guarded receptions, where the Kaiser and his wife were the guests of honour, would be totally impossible to enter without a surprise strategy. Therefore, before he could enjoy the splendour of the *Zwinger*, he had to trace the man he needed to create a diversion at the reception. Too dangerous to take a hansom, drivers would remember him, so he walked some distance to well-known stables.

Hiring a steed, he followed a bridle path until he came to an isolated cottage. Making sure no one had followed him he dismounted, approaching the cottage slowly, looking for all the world as if he were lost. No need to knock. A buxom, middle-aged woman, with fair hair, opened the door and stared at him for some moments. As soon as he asked for a stein of water she smiled, and showed him into a small room overlooking farmland. In the distance he could see a couple of lads tending a huge flock of sheep and a man who had obviously seen him arrive making his way to the cottage.

The woman, he never discovered her name, brought him a tankard of warm beer, proving that she had understood that *stein of water* was the password. Minutes later, Helstein, a well-built man with grey hair and piercing black eyes, entered the room. They talked for some fifteen minutes, during which time Holmes enlarged on his strategy for the diversion he needed to ensure that he could enter the reception at the *Wallpavilion* while the fracas ensued.

'How?' I asked Holmes, 'did you find the man?'

'By dredging my memory, Watson. It's strange how much we store, and how much can be retrieved. Years ago, more than I care to remember, Mycroft, as a young man went climbing in the Alps with a party of Germans. Their guide, whom everyone thought was German, was actually Swiss and has since been established as a farmer outside Dresden. A good cover. Always difficult to keep track of a farmer who can be attending to matters on his land or calling on neighbouring farms. Helstein's job was to keep his ear to the ground because the Swiss knew that both Germany and Austria planned to expand even further.'

'But Mycroft would never have gone climbing from choice.'

'You are right. He was there to make contact with Helstein, but as soon as the business was done he gave up the climbing, blaming it on a bad back.'

I have to say that for a few seconds I wondered whether Mycroft was a double agent before dismissing the idea as unworthy.

'Holmes, tell me, did the opera come up to expectations?'

'Yes, my dear friend, but with reservations. All I had to do was close my eyes and imagine that it was Richard Wagner conducting his own masterpiece.'

'Reservations! Then the theatre did not come up to expectations?'

'Oh, yes! A magnificent structure also known as the *Semperoper*, after its creator Gottfried Semper, who designed it twice.'

'Twice!'

'The first building burnt down in 1869 and the second one was completed in 1878. Let's hope it never happens again. At the end of the first act I opened my eyes and gazed round the theatre, in particular at the loges, where the aristocrats and their overdressed ladies were sitting. The Kaiser Wilhelm and his most attractive wife were in the royal box, but in the shadows behind the Kaiser I caught sight of a face I knew only too well. The Mephistophelian scoundrel who had brought about Mycroft's downfall.'

'Moriarty!'

'Indeed! He remained in the box during the interlude, almost hidden by a waiter who had been serving wine and who remained in attendance. Needless to say, the rest of the performance should have been a joy, but I had other thoughts in my head. At last I had confirmation that my journey to Dresden was not in vain.

The performance was so extraordinary that the curtain was raised and lowered a dozen times before the conductor and soloists obliged with an encore. I was impatient to make my way to the *Wallpavillon*, but sat applauding until my hands ached. As I left the theatre I saw Helstein in the shadows, dressed in such a slovenly manner that no guard would have allowed him into the reception. He nodded at me and I followed slowly in his wake amidst a vast crowd walking towards the pavilion. He chose to join the queue behind a tall, well-built man and his buxom wife, who was wearing a hat made of ostrich feathers that served as an adequate screen until he approached the main door. As expected, immaculately clad guards, who were enjoying the occasion, bowed and smiled to guests as they entered but immediately they noticed the way that Helstein was dressed, their mood changed, and they ordered him to leave. He ignored their orders, saying that he had lost his invitation. Such a clamour ensued that I was able to shake my head at one of the guards, who shrugged his shoulders and allowed me to pass without producing any evidence.

It was so warm in the pavilion that I was afraid that the slight scar I had implanted on the side of my face would melt. For safety's sake I withdrew and removed it. By the time the guests had imbibed quantities of superb Eiswein they were talking unrestrainedly about the riots and unrest in England. In one corner of the room they were even discussing the incarceration of a spy called Holmes and the state of the British monarchy. They asked my opinion about the state of affairs in the country but I made it clear that I was more interested in science than politics.

One of the guests suddenly asked me what I thought about the mind of a Kaiser who had been on the throne for barely two years and who, so it was said, had ambitions to stretch his empire even further. One of the men told him to keep quiet but I explained that I was a doctor, and everything I was told was always in confidence. They all relaxed and it was then that I heard another group behind me, discussing what they thought was a rumour. They were all laughing at the comic, who was telling them a tale about two armies that were being prepared to invade England. A clever strategy, roared one man, but utterly impossible because we have too many borders to guard, so how can we spare the troops? The narrator of the fabulous tale, a wishful thinker in my opinion, was not to be diverted. First of all, he told the assembled throng that the Kaiser who visited England at least twice a year to pay his respects to his grandmother, the Queen, would, on his next visit, arrive with a smartly dressed retinue of 200 men. They would disembark at Harwich, make their way to London where, amidst cheering crowds, they would march up Whitehall and the Mall towards Buckingham Palace to celebrate the Queen's birthday. However, before the contingent reached the palace, the crowd's mood would change and a carefully orchestrated demonstration would erupt. A rioting throng would demand the abdication of the queen, while at the same time welcoming the Kaiser as the next king.'

'But why, Holmes, were two armies being specially trained?'

'Propaganda, Watson. That's what I thought at the time. Nevertheless, after infiltrating the group behind me I asked a general, weighed down with medals and unsteady on his feet, to explain why such a dastardly strategy was necessary. It seems, and this I find hard to believe, that at the same time as the procession was wending its way up Whitehall an army would disembark at Harwich and another at Dover. In both towns, in which there is a great deal of poverty, the populace, after hearing town criers announcing that Victoria had been deposed, might even welcome their saviours with open arms.'

'Pipe dreams, Holmes! Our Navy would foil any such attempt.'

'Yes, but the ideas behind the Kaiser's visit are more substantial than any pipe dream. Like you, I have total faith in the ability of our Navy to foil any attempt at invasion, but the devious plot conceived for the Kaiser's next visit could bring down the monarchy. He wants to expand his empire. What better way than to topple Victoria? We know that she is a headstrong monarch who has been ill advised by those close to her, but her mourning must cease. She must be warned that there are pitfalls ahead unless she re-emerges as an Empress. Watson, there is no doubt that her wretched grandson, Wilhelm, sees himself as an Emperor in a position to take over the greatest empire the world has ever seen. Together with the German territories, he would be a formidable opponent.'

'Holmes,' I expostulated, there is no place in Great Britain for a German.'

'You forget, Watson, that for the past two centuries we have been ruled by Germans, by the House of Hanover.'

'But over the years they have become anglicised.'

'Precisely, which is why we must foil Moriarty's evil plans. It is he who, for his own devious ends, is now instrumental in filling the Kaiser's head with the right of succession.'

'The Hanover Club! That is where germination takes place.'

'And where it must not take root. The House of Hanover has become an institution, but because Prince Bertie married a Dane the genes grow weaker, one of the many facts that Moriarty may be sharing with the Kaiser.'

'Holmes, the whole idea is laughable. There is no way the Kaiser can conquer Britain. Napoleon, a brilliant general in the field failed in his attempt to cross the channel. Nelson put paid to all that. Holmes, I place my faith in our navy, a body of men that can face and destroy any foe. We must prevent this idea taking root, even if it means that you have to approach the Foreign Office.'

'No, Watson, we must leave well alone.'

'Holmes, what is happening to you? Do you not care that our country is threatened?'

'There would be no battle, my friend, just remember the Greeks came bearing gifts.'

'Blast the Greeks, I want to know how you are going to deal with the situation.'

'We know that the Kaiser is being ill-advised, but we must not interfere until Mycroft has regained his freedom.'

I could not believe what I was hearing.

'You look somewhat dazed, my friend, You must remember that in the past Mycroft has been privy to any events that could potentially destabilise the monarchy. We also know that as a detective, although lacking ambition, he has such extraordinary mental powers that only he will know how to deal with the machinations being fermented by Professor Moriarty. In the Kaiser's eyes this is an undertaking to dethrone the Queen, but in my eyes it has another truth.'

'You can't be serious, Holmes. All this to undermine you, to destroy your reputation!'

He nodded. I have to admit that at the time it struck me that all this business of assuming the role of a psychiatrist had undermined his own common sense approach. An approach that had sustained him in every case with which he had ever dealt.

CHAPTER FIFTEEN

It was a drear morning, clothed in such a thick pea-souper that even with the windows closed our lungs were affected. As I entered the room Holmes was coughing his heart out, but that, I have no doubt, could be blamed on the thick shag he was smoking. I was angry because, yet again, he had failed to share his plan of action with me. I sat down in silence, poured myself a cup of tea and settled down to eat my breakfast.

'Watson,' said Holmes softly, 'I must apologise for not keeping you in the picture, but like all artists, I am not happy with the brushwork. The background is too dark, the foreground unclear and the perspective badly drawn.'

'What, Holmes, is missing from this masterpiece of a canvas?'

'Your sarcasm is warranted, but let me go one step further. The picture is a triptych needing to be hinged together as one work of art. In one panel I see a man, woman and child entering a manor house. A servant is carrying their trunks. In the foreground a hansom is driving away and in the background are two men on horseback. One looking towards the house and the other staring at the foliage.'

'Holmes,' I gasped, as it dawned on me what the allusions were, 'you cannot do this. You will be sending Sir Henry Baskerville to his death.'

'We have to smoke Stapleton out by whatever means it takes.'

I was staggered. So tell me, Holmes, why was I not depicted on the unfinished canvas?'

'It is a narrative picture and it tells a story, but it is not easy to see a poacher hidden in the bushes with his shotgun at the ready.'

'It is utter madness, Holmes.'

'Not if you look clearly at the picture. The three people depicted live in the stable cottage at the rear of the manor house; Palmer, the groom, his wife and child. On arrival, after the sun has gone down, when even the most powerful binoculars would not be adequate to distinguish features, the Palmers, in the garb of gentry, will enter the house. Once inside they will, quite safely, assume their normal roles, but in the meantime, the assassin, believing that his intended target has returned, will bide his time. He is a patient man, an intelligent being, but not quite clever enough.'

'That is but one picture, Holmes. What of the others?'

'Ah! In the centre panel of the triptych you would recognise Whitehall, Parliament Square and many buildings in the background, all clouded in a grey mist, looking as if the picture needs cleaning. The third panel is a combination of two scenes. In the foreground a crowd is converging on Buckingham Palace, and in the background several horses are standing in front of a forbidding prison. When the triptych is closed each panel folds upon the other, all totally related.'

'How,' I asked, 'do these mind-pictures aid your strategy? To me it seems to make the problem more obscure.'

'No, Watson, even you must see the relationship!'

'What I do see, thankfully, is that those three dear people will be safe.'

'Providing, Watson, that you make no effort to visit them.'

'But Mary..........'

He interrupted. 'Telegraph her, say all is well but we are both being followed. She will understand. You could raise a few red herrings by ambling round Green Park and testing my assertions.'

Holmes was right. On gazing through the window I saw, through the fog, a bearded individual standing in the doorway of a shop, ostensibly reading a newspaper, but with his eyes fixed on 221B.

At that moment a cab pulled up outside the house and seconds later we heard the bell. 'We have a visitor, Holmes.'

'Did you see who it was?'

'No, merely that it was a tall male.'

'Too early for Lestrade,' said Holmes. 'He knows I am never dressed at this early hour.'

As I opened the door, curious to find out who was calling at such an hour, Mrs Hudson, who was halfway up the stairs, announced that Sir John Falconby was here to see Mr Holmes.

'Excellent,' exclaimed Holmes, 'show him in, Mrs Hudson, then clear away these breakfast dishes, if you please.'

Falconby entered, but remained silent until Mrs Hudson had cleared the dishes and I had closed the door. He then apologised to Holmes for intruding at such an unearthly hour, then sat down without being invited to do so. It was quite obvious to me that he was exhausted both mentally and physically.

Holmes stood for some minutes looking out of the window before turning to face Falconby. His next words would have been unbelievable had it not been Holmes uttering them.

'You are earlier then expected, Falcon. I thought you would take the ten o'clock express.'

Holmes had dropped a thunderbolt. Falconby gasped while I wondered what other information had not been divulged.

'You expected me?' He whispered.

Holmes nodded before asking me to pour our guest a brandy.

'How on earth did you know? What is going on, Homer?'

'You are going to tell me. However, let me say that you could do nothing until I returned from Dresden. Your orders must have been explicit. Nevertheless, you are disobeying the black king by playing a finesse,' said Holmes as he rose to take a look out of the window. 'You may not have much time, but it is imperative that you explain every act you have undertaken on behalf of Professor Moriarty.'

'All this, Homer, may be the end of me, but I cannot rest until I have righted the wrongs that all originated with....'

Holmes gave him no time to finish. 'You are, of course, about to refer to events prior to the Stifle Affair?'

Falconby stiffened. 'My God! If you know how many others could have reached the same conclusion?'

'You forget, Colonel, that we were once combatants. Now without wasting any more time, perhaps you had better explain why you have become a pawn in the Professor's game?'

'Very well, but as yet I have never set eyes on the gentleman.'

'Hardly an appellation for such an evil being, however, pray continue while Doctor Watson records events.'

'First of all, Homer, how in God's name did you hear about the Stifle Affair?'

'From a reliable contact in the Home Office.'

'I see. No need to elaborate. You must have been in touch with that traitor Boyce.'

Holmes looked at Falconby with the vestige of a smile on his face. 'Not directly. In order to protect you it is better that way.'

It was a long story of misconceptions, roguery, blackmail and extortion. A story that I will record in as few words as possible.

Falconby was a handsome fellow who would still attract the fair sex in London's high life, but he had been excommunicated, sent down to a lack-lustre official post where the nightlife consisted of making sure the prison was secured. For him escaping prisoners were a nightmare, but even worse were the demands made by the so-called gentleman he had never met.

His fall from grace began shortly after his marriage when his wife gave birth to twins, a weakly pair. Unlike most women of her class she preferred to nurse them herself, never trusting highly competent nurses. She eschewed the bright lights, and remained at home until the boys were sent to Charterhouse.

By this time Falconby had installed a most attractive redheaded mistress in a lavish apartment in Grosvenor Square. Mistresses are invariably more expensive to maintain and more demanding than wives. His mistress, Millicent Doby, who had a passion for emeralds, may have felt she had a short tenure as his favoured lady and was hoarding for leaner years to come. Who knows? A colonel's salary was not enough to fund heavy school fees, a wife and an extravagant mistress. He searched for other ways. After having no luck at the gambling table he needed to find some sort of business where quick money could be made. For a colonel in the cavalry horses had always been a part of his life, therefore, it was not surprising that the Turf provided the answer.

On his small estate outside Godalming he kept two horses, tended by the man who also served as his gardener, but in order to enter the racing world he needed a loan of huge proportions to develop the stables and employ experienced grooms and stable lads. Maria, believing that he had left his mistress, persuaded her father to advance the necessary funding.

The plan took fifteen months to come to fruition by which time he became a relatively small player in the racing world. He achieved a certain measure of success by winning many minor events but he never managed a win in the major races. The income covered the outgoings, but unknown to his wife he still maintained the establishment in Grosvenor Square.

Maria may have been unaware of the situation, but not her father, who, after a tempestuous meeting with his son-in-law in a private room at the Athenaeum, demanded his money back with interest. Unknown to Falconby, one of the members, who may have been standing on the balcony outside the room, heard every word. The facts were reported to the criminal who controlled the underworld. Shortly afterwards he received a missive from M, an initial that meant nothing to him. In the note M offered to settle all his debts provided he sacked his present stable staff and took on board a new crew, all had to be men he suggested.

Falconby said he was far from happy with this arrangement but he had no alternative. The change of staff was effective. He won many major races and at long last was accepted by the public and the Chairman of the Racing Board as a force to be reckoned with. He had repaid his father-in-law's loan, kept on the establishment in Grosvenor Square and to the amazement of his wife, spent more time at home. At the time he could not understand why M never contacted him again to collect the thousands he was owed.

Early one morning he arrived unexpectedly at the stables and standing in the shadows, he saw one of the stable lads holding a pot of black paint, while a groom with paintbrush in hand painstakingly disguised all the white markings on the horse's hind quarters.

At this point Holmes interrupted the flow. 'From this moment you realised you were powerless to escape from a well engineered trap.' Falconby nodded. 'The skulduggery continued, but you made no move to put paid to the practice. You were affluent, secure, so you thought, but you must have known that a time bomb was ticking away.'

'Of course I did, but what could I do? My whole world would have collapsed. I would have been court-martialled, then imprisoned in the very place I now command. I could not put my family through such stigma.'

'You would have won a small fortune, not far short of 4000 guineas had the heavens not opened. Zeus, who had been disguised to look like Adamant, won at Newmarket, fooling everyone until the rain came. However, you escaped lightly, did you not?'

'You seem to know so much, Homer, so why should I say more?'

'Professor Moriarty made sure that the ringer and the stable lads took the blame. No doubt he paid them well. A few months in gaol then out again, to continue with this nefarious practice in another corner of the globe.'

'You are right, Holmes. All engineered by the man on whom I have never set eyes.'

'However, probably owing much to your bravery in the First Boer War, you were found not guilty on all counts. Nevertheless, Field Marshal Grant made sure that you were never again admitted to the higher echelons of army tactical planning by posting you to a job no one would accept. You, of course, had no alternative.'

'Homer, before I explain why I desperately need your help. You have to realise that your brother is innocent and that I had no hand in the vile plot to bring him down.'

Holmes nodded, saying nothing for several minutes while he replenished his pipe. It was impossible to distinguish his facial expression behind the smoke screen he had created, but I could see from the way Falconby sat fidgeting that the Governor was a frightened man.

At last, as the mist cleared, Holmes, looking at Falconby, half smiled. 'Of course my brother is innocent. No one in either the Home Office or the Foreign Office can match his devotion to Queen and country, but you know that. You were, for a brief spell, given a responsible job in the Home Office and your paths, no doubt, crossed.'

'Yes, we crossed swords at several round table discussions all in aid of ensuring that *Bloody Sunday* never happened again.'

'You were too successful, Falcon. Means had to be devised to get rid of you. What better way than to make sure the horse was only disguised with a thin layer of paint? Paint that should have dripped off when the horse sweated, but failed to do so. In fact the plan nearly came to naught. For the instigator of the plot, rain was an unexpected blessing.

The ringer, who had been well paid, always knew that he would have to serve time but never for one moment did Moriarty expect you to be cleared of the offence. While at the Home Office you were a constant danger, a man with the ability to put paid to many of the demonstrations he had planned in the capital. You were too professional, far-sighted, and adept at organising the troops, but Moriarty made no allowance for your gallantry in the field. That was his undoing. Even an evil genius can make errors of judgement.'

'You are right, Homer, had it not been for the first all-out fight with the Boers I would have paid the penalty. But it is not the past but the future that we should be discussing. I need your advice, for I have no idea what this fiend has in store for me nor by what Machiavellian means he planted Henderson in the prison to keep a constant watch on me. The man never went on holidays. In fact, it was unusual for the Chaplain ever to leave the place for more than a few hours at a time. I always believed it was a chance meeting when we sat next to each other at morning service at St Leonard's Church. At the time it seemed like the Lord's doing. It was only when we found that he had fled the prison hospital and half-killed a man in the process, that I realised how foolish I had been.'

'You were indeed,' said Holmes, not mincing matters. 'At lunch not so long ago you said you were a good character reader.'

'I believed his story. A dying wife! A still-birth! It explained why the man had to escape from such heartrending memories. One thing, I have to admit, puzzled me.

All the previous vicars at St Leonard's Church had been quite happy to exchange pulpits once every few years but Henderson wanted to stay put.'

Someone,' I said, 'might have been tempted to look him up in Crockfords, then the fat would have been in the fire.'

'You are right, Doctor Watson, but it will never happen again. Next time I shall expect excellent references, even if it means weeks without a chaplain.'

Falconby was stunned when he learnt that Henderson had already been responsible for two deaths at Baskerville Hall; first Sir Charles, then the wretched convict, but by far the most heinous crime was the murder he committed on the Paddington express after he made his escape from the area. Falconby sat shaking his head, finding it hard to believe that the Reverend Jonathan Williams, who had visited the prison on many occasions, had been stripped of his clothes, robbed of all his possessions and until recently had been buried in a pauper's grave.

'It could be even worse than that,' gasped Falconby. 'Do you remember that when we lunched at the Vicarage I told you that my previous chaplain had been killed?'

Holmes nodded. 'We have reached the same conclusion. The Chaplain was killed on Moriarty's orders to make way for Stapleton, who was then calling himself Henderson. You even mentioned at the luncheon that it was difficult to find staff. He is a clever man who will now assume another guise but, Falcon, you can do your part in discovering his whereabouts.'

How do I set about that?'

'I believe you mentioned that Stapleton, Henderson as you remember him, tried to spend ten to fifteen minutes each week with some of the worst offenders in an effort to persuade them to admit to their perfidy and pray to their Maker for pardon.'

'That is the case.'

There will be malefactors with whom he spent more than fifteen minutes, even seeing them on a daily basis.'

'I get the drift, Homer. You are saying that two or three of the worst offenders, including the felon who was killed when feeding the hound, may have aided and abetted him in whatever nefarious deed he was planning.'

'Yes, Falcon, your words echo my thoughts. We do need to discover his whereabouts.'

'It seems obvious to me, Holmes,' I said, butting in quickly, 'that he will lie low, remaining in the area. As a lepidopterist he knows the area like the back of his hand, and would be able to hide on the moor for weeks on end without being seen.'

Holmes chuckled. 'I was successful, Watson, because when hunting for Sir Charles's murderer I made sure that a young man delivered the necessities of life daily.'

'I see what you are saying, Holmes. Not only will he need nourishment but a complete change of clothes is a must before he can emerge unnoticed and set foot anywhere near Baskerville Hall. He could kill again, of course. Any unsuspecting walker on the moors is at risk.'

'No, Watson, I think not. Far too dangerous to leave a stream of clues in his wake. We forget we are dealing with a thespian. This time, I think, we will be looking for a beardless man whose hair is a different colour, whose accent is local or maybe Welsh, who wears spectacles and sports a broad brimmed hat to throw shadows over his face.'

Falconby looked puzzled. 'But, Homer, how and where would he live?'

'Think, Falcon, think! He has so few options. What would you do? Would you find a farmer who desperately needs labourers and can offer the warmth of a barn in which to sleep, or would you opt for the mines where the work is dangerous, where men die or are permanently injured, where you would never see the light of day?'

'There is no choice. Farm labouring is the answer.'

'There you have it,' said Holmes, as he rose to peer through the window. 'He would be well fed and sleep in a barn. Nothing easier.'

'Not easy,' I said. 'First of all he has to find clothes, then a farmer in dire need.'

Holmes totally ignored me. He was obviously many steps ahead.

'Falcon,' he said abruptly, ' return to Princeton, speak to the inmates with whom Stapleton had the most contact, especially those who were born and bred in this part of the world. He will have made sure that he had an escape route if his plans went awry. He will have learned which farmer would probably give him food and shelter in return for free labour. He will now be hidden away, adapting himself to his new surroundings while plotting how to kill Sir Henry.'

'Why on earth is this his *raison d'être*?' Falconby was incredulous.

'He has to kill Sir Henry in order to make sure his son Arthur succeeds to the title and estate.'

'What are you saying, Homer? It sounds ridiculous, like castles in Spain.'

'No, there is nothing ridiculous about his quest. I have established that Stapleton is indeed a Baskerville and should have inherited the title when Sir Charles died, but Stapleton's father, a ne'er-do-well who fathered a host of illegitimate off-springs, was disinherited. Sir Charles may have had no knowledge of his nephew's existence or if he had, did not want to risk an illegitimate successor.'

For nearly ten minutes neither man spoke. It was obvious to me that Holmes was waiting for Falconby to come to terms with a state of affairs of which he had known nothing.

Eventually, Holmes half-smiled at Falconby. 'I know what you are thinking, my friend, and you are right. It is more important at this moment to work behind the scenes for Mycroft's release. Only he has the power and know-how to prevent a disastrous riot occurring when the Kaiser next visits the capital.'

'Too many violent incidents these days,' growled Falconby as he refilled his pipe.

Holmes sat down in the window-seat and held out his hands as if in supplication. 'This is different. The riot Moriarty has planned is the culmination of many carefully orchestrated demonstrations in various parts of the country. This time, as I learnt in Dresden recently, the Kaiser and his vast entourage will make their way down the Mall towards the palace, where thousands will be cheering the Kaiser and demanding the abdication of the Queen.'

'Impossible! Preposterous!' roared Falconby.

'No, I am afraid not. Mycroft must be released. You and I must work towards that end. We have a mole in the Home Office who will divulge the names of those who have total belief in my brother's innocence, but so far we only know the identity of one man in the Home Office who is aiding and abetting Moriarty.'

'Then he must be unmasked.'

'There will be others,' I said, 'who will take over.'

'I am sure you are right, Doctor. But Homer, is it not possible that the catalyst who engineered my downfall is in charge of the Record Office?'

'Quad erat demonstrandum, Falcon. He is, without doubt, the only man who could have set up the trap to net Mycroft. The only man with access to the files that were so conveniently discovered in the early hours of the morning.'

I suggested that Sir John called on Dr Breucot once again to ask him for a further report on Mycroft's mental state and whether he could assess whether his patient was innocent or guilty.

'Innocent! Of course he's innocent,' yelled Falconby, 'I have made that clear in reports to the Minister, but I will do as you suggest, Doctor. In fact, would you get in touch with him immediately, and ask whether he would be prepared to return to Princeton with me on the next express?'

Holmes, with an almost imperceptible shake of the head, told me all I needed to know.

'He's a busy man, Falcon. His appointment book will be full. Why not do as I have suggested and speak with the inmates who had contact with Stapleton? In the meantime I will call on Dr Breucot and explain the seriousness of the situation in the hope that he will be able to advise us on what further action to take.'

Falconby, silent for a couple of minutes, suddenly jumped to his feet, saying he had a brief call to make before catching the early afternoon express.

'Hadn't you better share your thoughts,' murmured Holmes, 'about how you plan to become more involved in events?'

'How do you know that I intend to become more involved? No. Don't answer that. You were always one step ahead when it came to lunge and parry.'

'You are urgently needed in the capital, Falcon. You know that. Your expertise in dealing with riots and exposing ringleaders who have caused so much mayhem in the past is unmatched.'

'You have my word, Homer, that I will worm my way back. I have decided that once Mycroft has been exonerated I will most certainly be back.'

Holmes smiled. 'You will, no doubt, before catching the express, call on your mother, a frail lady in her nineties, and prepare her for the next scene in the action.'

'Not frail, Homer, a healthy strong-minded woman who will never admit her age but.....'

'But,' interrupted Holmes, 'one who despite her fitness will suffer the effects of a slight heart attack, enough to bring her eldest son rushing up to the Great Wen.'

Sir John laughed. 'Once again you are a step ahead. Princeton won't suffer. My deputy is an admirable chap whom I hope one day, in the not too distant future, will replace me.'

185

'Surely,' I asked, 'you won't be leaving Princeton until you have definite proof of Stapleton's whereabouts?'

'It won't take an unconscionable time. There are ways and means, doctor, which I am sure you would rather not know about. We all want to see this villainous creature arrested, charged and hanged, but you have such expertise in these matters, Homer, that I will tread warily. If we are to protect Sir Henry Baskerville, timing is all. Now about Boyce, who should have been hanged for treason, have you anyone, Homer, who can keep track of him and his associates until my return?'

'Tracking his movements in the capital is no problem, but he is weaving his way, I suspect, into elite circles where he can inauspiciously spread his propaganda. That is why we need Mycroft on board.'

'Maybe,' I said slowly, 'Dr Breucot might be able to assist us?'

'Oh no, Watson,' riposted Holmes as he winked at me, 'Dr Breucot is a psychologist, a medical man, not an infiltrator. In fact, Watson, it might not come amiss if you and I make a flying visit to Baskerville Hall tomorrow to.....'

'Holmes,' interrupted Falconby, 'as I already have Dr Breucot's diagnosis, it would be much more to the point if you could talk to your brother, but there will be no record in my appointment book that you have even visited the prison.'

'Very well, Falcon,' replied Holmes, after a considerable pause. 'Watson and I will board the midday express tomorrow, giving you sufficient time to interrogate any of the convicts you think may have been working hand in glove with Stapleton.'

186

'Now, gentlemen I must call a cab, pay my respects to my mother, who lives in Westbourne Drive and may be ailing any day now. I will remain overnight and return to the fortress early in the morning.' He shook hands, with us both, nodded to Holmes saying he now had a purpose in life, and thus he left Baker Street a much happier man than when he entered.

CHAPTER SIXTEEN

For the first time since Mycroft's unlawful arrest, a term my friend used constantly, Holmes was unusually buoyant. The fact that Sir John intended to make every effort to have Mycroft released, trace Stapleton's whereabouts and then by subterfuge return to the capital, gave great impetus to the case.

During the day, however, Holmes was exceedingly restless, spending two hours walking round Regent Park, no doubt planning a strategy for obtaining a pardon for Mycroft in the forthcoming week. At the time I thought it a fruitless exercise and felt he would have been better advised to have spent the time tracking down Boyce's associates.

Shortly before dinner Mrs Hudson bustled in to ask whether we wished to delay the evening meal until after Holmes had had words with another visitor, who was quite prepared to return in an hour or so.

Needless to say the visitor, who happened to be Evans, was more important than sustenance. Mrs Hudson, showing no surprise at the decision, made it clear that the Irish stew, one of my favourite dishes, would not suffer if the gentleman caller was gone in half an hour.

A tired looking Evans could hardly wait to impart his information but Holmes insisted that he sat down, got his breath back, had a beer, then told us all. Unusual, I must say, for Holmes, who was bursting to hear what the man had to say, but it was obvious that Evans, who was taking his job as an inside man very seriously, couldn't contain himself.

On hearing that one of the cleaners responsible for Charles Boyce's department had slipped and broken two fingers, Evans had volunteered to cover for him, making the excuse that with a young family he had many unexpected expenses.

Mycroft's office, we learned, had not been occupied since his abrupt departure. Nevertheless, it was cleaned at an early hour every evening, giving Evans a chance to slip in during the small hours. Evans also told us that Boyce was never seen in Mycroft's office. It was Macey, his assistant, who was constantly in and out collecting and delivering files and sealed packages.

According to the porter at the *Diogenes*, Boyce, to many of the members, was a joker who was in charge of filing and keeping under lock and key a quantity of paper best used as kindling. Holmes disagreed. That man, he told me, shortly after my first visit to the *Diogenes*, has his fingers on everything of importance that is happening in this country. Who better to do lasting harm? Holmes was right. To incriminate Mycroft all Boyce had to do was extract highly secret case-papers on *The Ripper Case* and have Macey plant them in Mycroft's office, together with hand-outs inciting the man-in-the-street to demonstrate against the monarchy in an anarchic uprising.

Evans had taken the opportunity to search through drawers and cabinets in Boyce's office. He found nothing that he thought could be of any use, but the treasure he produced had not been hidden. Lying on top of the desk was a spectacle case and an apparently harmless leather-bound address book that Evans, just in the nick of time, slipped into his pocket before a guard entered to check that cleaning had been completed regarding all the file repositories in the adjoining offices. Thankfully Evans made his escape and mingling with a host of cleaners, left the building in the early hours.

By the time Big Ben struck three he was back at home, but before turning in he decided to glance through the address book.

'Much like any other address, book, sir,' he told Holmes as he handed it over.

My friend, I have to say, virtually grabbed it and spent the next ten minutes humming to himself as he thumbed through several pages.

'This, Watson,' he enthused, 'is not just gold dust, this is a veritable Eldorado. It can only have been left on the desk by chance. Maybe Boyce, who was wearing his spectacles, had an urgent message to meet one of the anarchists? On his way out, he hurriedly picked up his cigars, but left the spectacle case and this incriminating evidence behind? Easily done.'

'But you have never met him, Holmes, how do you know about the cigars and the spectacle case?'

'Smell the book, Watson, he smokes only the best.'

'And the spectacle case? He was not wearing spectacles when I saw him at the *Diogenes*.'

'Vanity, old chap, vanity. Some of the names and addresses in this book have been writ so large that he could easily decipher them without a visual aid. Had this book been misplaced it would have meant nothing to the finder, but it has a strange truth of its own.

'And what's in that book, Mr Holmes?' asked Evans, who was intrigued.

'There are several names in this book that are coded in an almost childlike manner. In the first vowel of the name or address a miniscule dot is visible, almost as if the pen had slipped. Evans,' said Holmes, who was euphoric, 'has provided the names and addresses of the plotters. Evans is our Tresham.'

I have to say that both Evans and I looked at Holmes in amazement.

'No need to look so amazed, Watson. It was Tresham who divulged the names of those involved in the *Gunpowder Plot*, another plot against the monarchy.

Evans looked pleased. His night's work not in vain, but there was even more to come.

'It is probably of no interest, Mr Holmes, but I managed to sneak into Mr Mycroft's office, but it was a waste of time. You see, sir, because the office has not been occupied since he left, I found nothing of interest, but it was strange to see Mr Holmes' hat and coat still hanging on the coat stand. Almost as though he had never left.'

'Ah!' said my friend pressing the tips of his fingers together, 'there, for sure, is my *raison d'être*, my way into the establishment.'

He wrenched a drawer out of the bureau, and turned it upside down, scattering the contents on his desk. After a frantic search, he yelled 'Eureka!' as he pulled out three papers covered in diagrams.

Totally bemused, I asked why were three rough looking sheets of diagrams of use to him.

'A simple ruse, Watson, as good as any password. My way to gain entry to the Home Office and, hopefully, to have words with Sir Giles Hipkiss, the present Director of Administration.' He folded the papers, placed them in an envelope, addressed them to Mycroft, then carefully placed the envelope in tissue paper.

'Evans,' he said, speaking softly, 'I am relying on you to place the envelope in an inside pocket in my brother's coat now hanging in his office. Wear gloves. Make sure you do not handle it.'

'How does this help, sir?' asked Evans, now totally bewildered.

'These are important documents that I have mislaid, possibly sent to my brother, but essential if I am to solve a problem that has been besetting me for so long.'

'Very well, sir, it shall be done,' smiled Evans, now no longer the tired looking man who had limped into the room.

Over dinner I asked Holmes what he hoped to achieve.

'A legitimate excuse, Watson, giving me cause to call at the Home Office, see Sir Giles Hipkiss, and ask if I might take a brief look in Mycroft's office for an important document that might help to solve a case. They will, of course, have been through the office with a toothcomb, but one careless fellow could have missed an envelope in an inside pocket.'

'Which case, Holmes, are you hoping to solve?'

'You are slow today, Watson. I need to prove that Mycroft was unlawfully arrested. Only by talking to Hipkiss, who was at university with me, can I hope to prove that everything Mycroft has striven for in life has been for Queen and country.'

Halfway through our meal, and soon after Evans had departed, I received a telegram from Mary, asking me to return to Paddington as soon as possible. Nothing for it but to go home that evening. So many eventualities went through my mind. Was Mary under the weather again, was the child ill, or had Stapleton been seen in the vicinity? Holmes advised me not to dither but to call a cab and make haste.

On arrival Mary hugged me so tightly that one would have thought that I had returned from the North Pole after a long absence. There was nothing wrong with young Arthur, who was fast asleep clutching a rag doll. He certainly did not need medication nor did Sir Henry or Beryl Stapleton, who both looked in the best of health. Mary thrust a whisky into my hand and I sat down, looking at the three of them. What was going on? Mary shrugged slightly and nodded her head towards Sir Henry. At last he came to the point.

Watson,' he said without preamble, 'we will be returning to Baskerville tomorrow.'

'But,' I gasped, 'that is madness. You cannot return until Stapleton has been apprehended.'

'Beryl and I have discussed the matter. I am not going to put the lives of my servants at risk by allowing them to take part in a charade that Holmes thought might act as an enticement, in other words, a sprat to catch a mackerel. The charade cannot go ahead. They are good people.'

'If you are adamant, why not leave Mrs Stapleton and young Arthur with my wife? At least they would have the protection of our London police.'

'Oh no, Doctor Watson,' said Beryl Stapleton. 'If Sir Henry returns then I shall be with him, so too will Arthur. We will take great care and thankfully all the servants, who are trustworthy, will keep their eyes open. At least they know what my husband looks like.'

'What he looked like,' I said correcting her. 'Remember he is a past master of disguise. How else did he manage to pick Arthur up and pat his head when he fell in the market place?'

She paled at this. 'That's impossible!'

She shook her head, but it was all too obvious that she was not going to change her mind. She had no intention of leaving the man she had come to love. The carefully laid plans Holmes had predicted in the imaginary triptych were not going according to plan.

'All right,' I conceded. 'Holmes and I have decided to visit Princeton tomorrow. We will all travel to Exeter on the midday train, but before calling at the prison, Holmes and I will accompany you to Baskerville Hall. We will alight first, and check that there are no strangers in the area, making it safe for you to enter the house.' Now, I thought, what else would Holmes have suggested? Ah yes. 'Do not,' I said, ' send a wire to the house. Arrive out of the blue so to speak.'

'Too late, Watson, I sent a wire this afternoon. Only fair to give the servants time to prepare.'

On my return to Baker Street, Holmes, who, much to my chagrin, had never shared his thoughts on Baskerville's short stay in London was not in the least surprised that Sir Henry had decided to return.

'It's the only way, Watson, that we can trap Stapleton, but Baskerville must be warned to stay in the grounds with staff in attendance and never walk on the moors.'

'Have you forgotten the child?' I asked angrily. 'He could be kidnapped.'

'No, Arthur will not be kidnapped. Stapleton's ambition is to see his son succeed to the title. Kidnapping the child will impede progress. Only murder will achieve his objective.'

'Now, Holmes, we have to rely on Falconby to wave his wand and produce the rabbit.'

'You could say that, my friend!'

The following day, together with Sir Henry, Beryl and young Arthur, Holmes and I caught the express to Exeter. It was a pleasurable journey, with the child asking a myriad of questions, which Holmes took great delight in answering, while Sir Henry dozed and I read.

Sir Henry, ignoring my advice on the advisability of hiring a cab at the station, had wired the Hall and asked Palmer to bring the coach that was waiting when we arrived. Sir Henry picked up the child and with Beryl leading the way, clambered into the wagon while Holmes and I brought up the rear, making sure that no one seemed particularly interested in our arrival.

It was a pleasant homecoming for Beryl and Sir Henry, but not so pleasant for young Arthur, who wanted to run straight outside and fly his kite, but Holmes was adamant that the child had to be confined for a day or two while we called at Princeton to check out Stapleton's possible whereabouts with Falconby.

CHAPTER SEVENTEEN

Sir John had no difficulty in persuading his mother, a lady of great perspicacity, into becoming another piece in the great game. A pawn only, he had said, but one whose moves could threaten the black king.

On arriving back at Princeton his first action had been to inspect all belongings that Stapleton had left behind. There were a couple of books on natural phenomena and Lepidoptera, a good hunter, still ticking, and a small notebook. The cheap, well-handled notebook proved to be of inestimable worth, for in it Stapleton had noted down the day and time he had interviewed men serving life sentences. Only one of the men, James MacDowell, had escaped but died shortly after being badly mauled by the beast whilst attempting to feed the brute. His dying words were *enders, enders* a lead to the identification of Henderson.

There were three constantly recurring names. Falconby, when interrogating the men did no more, so he said, than threaten them with ten more years in the quarries, where they would be stone-breaking twenty hours a day, not the usual ten. One man, after several sessions with Stapleton, had found peace by confessing to his felony, proving that the bogus chaplain's work had not been in vain. The other two thugs of the first order were prepared to talk, but only after they had been told that the ex-chaplain would never know who had grassed.

One man convicted of arson, who had burnt down a barn in order to distract the farmer while he continued his nefarious activities of sheep stealing, came clean. He gave Falconby the locations of several farms in villages north of

Worcester, where there was always work and sleeping accommodation in rainproof barns. Reeves, who had been incarcerated for attempting to murder his wife, took longer to break down. Only after two officers placed him in chains while Falconby promised him that he would never be free of the stricture, did he open his mouth. To Falconby's ears what the man said was not much help, could have been truth, could have been fiction, but for Holmes it was music. Reeves had been a schoolteacher in Bath and latterly Bristol. During his sessions with Stapleton they had discussed schools in both cities. The prisoner, prior to his ill-judged attempt at murdering his wife, had taught mathematics at the cathedral school in Bristol.

Holmes told Falconby that this made more sense. Stapleton was not the type to endure ten hours hard labour a day and be treated as a peasant. For the role of a teacher he had no need to act, because prior to moving to Merripit House on the Baskerville estate he had been known as Vandeleur, the headmaster and owner of St Oliver's private school in York. There had been an outbreak of diphtheria at the school, during which so many children had been taken ill that the school was forced to close down. A past master of disguise, he then changed his name to Stapleton before moving to Grimpen Mire. It was Stapleton who first discovered an unusual specimen of Lepidoptera that became known as the *Vandeleur Moth*.

Falconby was not at all happy at Baskerville's return, but Holmes thought that while Stapleton was teaching some distance away, it would be safe for Sir Henry to move freely during the day.

'One thing worries me, Falcon.'

'And that is?'

'Stapleton would not have gone so far afield unless he had an informant at Baskerville Hall who could make sure he knew when the so-called holiday ended and when his wife and son were expected back at the Hall.'

It suddenly dawned on me that Stapleton would have a perfect alibi, provided he never missed any classes.

Holmes agreed. 'You are right, Watson. Travelling from Bristol to the estate would ostensibly only be feasible at weekends and holidays, unless during the dark hours he sought a strong mount and rode here.'

'But, Homer, we have to find out what sort of guise the man has taken on, the colour of his hair, whether he has a beard or has adopted characteristics he never used or needed as a chaplain.'

'Maybe I can help?' Falconby crossed the room and from a large cabinet extracted several files. 'These files contain the addresses of all my officers who have recently retired. I know for certain that two of them are living in Bristol.'

'Excellent work, Falcon.' Holmes brightened quite considerably. 'It would only need two men to cover the area, call at every school in Bristol with an excuse that they are looking for a distant cousin who may have been taken on the staff recently.'

'Ah!' grunted Falconby, 'Smith is precisely the man we need. A born busybody who never missed anything that went on in the prison. I always thought he had extraordinary vision and hearing. Now,' he said, after flicking through the files again, 'what about Baines? Yes, he should do. He is nowhere as nosy as Smith, more an uncle type who could wander around looking quite lost. The men used to be fooled by him, thinking him a bit of an idiot but he's nobody's idiot.'

'Two men,' agreed Holmes, ' who, if willing, would leave us free to deal with other matters.'

'Now, that we have solved the problem, Homer, you have the choice. You can talk privately with your brother in his cell or we can have a general discussion here in my office.'

There was no hesitation. Holmes, who knew he would be relying on his old sparring partner, said he preferred a general discussion.

Whilst waiting for Mycroft to appear, Falconby poured four robust whiskies and sat back at his desk with a half smile playing over his face. He looked so relaxed that it was hard to believe that this was the same man who only the day before had been a nervous wreck when he called at Baker Street.

An officer opened the door, ushering Mycroft into the office. He looked considerably thinner, and had lost much of his hair, but his demeanour told me that he was in a fighting mood, ready to take on all comers.

Falconby asked Holmes to open the batting by describing, in detail, his recent visit to Dresden, concentrating on the coup being planned for July during the Kaiser's visit. Mycroft listened in silence, nodding his head from time to time. Only when Falconby and Holmes both aired the view that every effort must be made to get him back to the capital as expeditiously as possible, did Mycroft react. Shaking his head, he made it clear that getting him back to the Home

Office was not the answer. If he showed his face all those involved in the plot would go underground.

'There is only one way, gentlemen,' said Mycroft, looking at us each in turn. 'I have to remain here. No point in scattering the vermin. We are all aware that the *modus operandi* was hatched in Dresden by Moriarty but the battle will be master-minded from within the Hanover Club. What you have to do is persuade one of the most trustworthy men in the Home Office to join the club. He must appear to be totally immersed in the business of ridding the country of the monarch, but at the same time tread warily. Whoever has the courage to step into the vipers' den could well risk everything he has striven for by losing his political status, or even worse, being knifed in the back.'

'Whom do you suggest? asked Falconby.

'Difficult to pinpoint the right fellow. On the face of it Boyce looked eminently trustworthy, so too did Macey but I have had plenty of time over the past few weeks to deliberate on the matter and there were pointers I had missed. What you really need to read is the full report on the committee meeting chaired by the Minister following my arrest. *Sub rosa*, of course! The papers will be under lock and key in the record office, only Boyce and the Director having access.'

A slight wink from Holmes in my direction indicated that he thought otherwise.

'The report,' continued Mycroft, 'will state quite clearly those who, serving on the committee, believed in my innocence, and those who believed in my guilt. A vote will have been taken – the matter will not have gone before a judge – the decision had to be immediate. Had it been processed formally, the whole country would once again have been focussing on the Ripper Case.'

'Supposing,' mused Falconby, 'that we manage to lay hands on this report. We may find four or five chaps believing in your innocence. What then?'

'Only one man should join. Two or three would be suspect, but shortly after, the man chosen for the diversion, having his feet firmly under the table, and knowing that the cabal has accepted him, must suggest that they might consider admitting a close personal associate whose views mirrored their own, an acquaintance who might well prove of inestimable service to the cause. Once he has the thumbs up he can then introduce a man who can watch his back, but it will be a dangerous situation, needing courage and total commitment.'

'First,' said Falconby,' we have to make contact with a monarchist whom we know to be trustworthy and who can keep his counsel. May not be so easy.'

'Leave it with me.' Holmes was decisive. 'By the end of the week I will have seen a copy of the committee report.'

Mycroft laughed. 'Well done, little brother! Now for another important matter, did you bring me a box of my favourite cigars?'

Without a word, Holmes waved his hands in the air before producing a box of Cuban from an inner pocket. We all roared with laughter.' Almost as good,' said Falconby, 'as a front seat at the Palladium.'

Mycroft took the proffered box and once he had lit up, told us in a much more serious vein that there was very little time to deal with the situation. 'There are twenty-four cigars in this box and I shall ration myself to two a day. The problem must have been dealt with before the box is empty.'

'Twelve days, brother,' murmured Holmes. 'Why is it you always give me the most difficult theorems to prove?'

'Because, Sherlock, you could not exist unless you had obscure cases to solve.'

'There is no doubt that the threat to the monarchy is the most serious business that I have ever had to face.'

'Remember,' brother, that there have been five attempts on Her Majesty's life, supposedly from mad men, but how do we know that they were not orchestrated by the Kaiser's secret police, of whom we know so little?'

'This time, Mycroft, we know the coup has been carefully planned by my arch rival.'

Falconby was taken by surprise 'Surely, Homer, you are not talking about Professor Moriarty?' Holmes nodded. 'How did he manage to get the ear of the Kaiser, and did you hear or see anything of him in Dresden?'

'He had gone to earth but his name was mentioned, and sanctioned, by those closest to the Kaiser. I doubt if Wilhelm may have had some slight idea that this malevolent coup was not dreamt up, in its entirety, by his sycophants, but by that odious professor I crossed swords with at university. The Kaiser, like his grandmother, the Queen, will be taken by surprise, but their reactions will be totally dissimilar.

Victoria will be horrified; Wilhelm will be pleased his dream of ruling the British Empire is about to be realised.'

Not,' pointed out Mycroft, 'if you hoist sail now and make headway.'

You could say that Mycroft gave us our marching orders, but I had to make sure that he did not require any medication.

'No, Watson,' he was quite emphatic, 'but a more comfortable bed would not come amiss.'

'Consider it done,' roared Falconby, ' and enjoy another whisky while the problem is being dealt with.'

'Another matter we must briefly discuss before you leave,' said Mycroft, as he rose to his feet.

Holmes and I looked at each other in astonishment. What had we not said? What had we missed?

'I take it, Sherlock that you will be staying at Baskerville Hall tonight?'

'We are.'

'Then take the opportunity to trace the spy before it is too late.'

'Telepathy, my dear fellow! Trace the spy! That was a decision I made during our journey down.'

'Holmes,' I ejaculated angrily, 'what are you both talking about? This is the first I have heard about a spy.'

'Apologies, my dear fellow, I should have mentioned the matter before, but we must ask ourselves why did the chaplain send a convict to feed the beast on the very night that Lestrade and his posse were all set to arrest him?'

Then and only then did the sequence of events become clear to me. Stapleton had been forewarned about the plan to arrest him, and knowing that the dog would never accept another handler he imagined that the convict would have been killed by the time the police struck, but it didn't quite work out that way. Fortunately Stapleton would never know that the wretched convict virtually gave the game away when he managed to whisper *enders....enders.*

'Are you implying, Holmes, that one of Sir Henry's servants kept Stapleton in the picture?'

'Yes, a man or boy was being paid to keep an eye on his wife and son. Whilst the proprieties were being observed, Beryl Stapleton was safe, but had she stepped out of line her days were numbered.'

The matter of the spy was solved, not by Holmes, but by Sir Henry. He called his staff together and made it patently clear that whoever was putting lives at risk had better come clean before he called the police.

It was obvious from the outset that only one servant appeared to be affected, a stable lad called Tommy Hart, who couldn't look Baskerville in the face and who kept his eyes firmly fixed on the tiled floor in the hall. Dismissing the rest of the staff, Sir Henry ordered the lad to remain. It was all a matter of pounds, shillings and pence and hungry mouths to feed. Tommy's father had been killed in a mining accident, leaving his wife with seven small children to feed and no income.

Late one night, Stapleton, who had caught Tommy netting pheasant, a crime in the eyes of many landowners, had threatened the lad with exposure unless he kept him informed about everything that went on in the Hall. Tommy, who was walking out with the kitchen maid, was instructed to listen to all the tittle-tattle, ask pertinent questions and report back.

Sir Henry graciously forgave the lad, and for his own sake had him moved to stables closer to his mother's cottage, but Holmes was not so generous. He wanted to know the time and place of the next rendezvous with Stapleton. Strangely, it was at a hideaway Holmes knew well, the very cave in which he had hidden nearly two years ago. If asked questions about Stapleton's wife and son, Tommy was to make it clear that Beryl Stapleton was merely the housekeeper and that Arthur was kept safe at all times. Holmes told the boy that if Stapleton failed to appear he must leave a note in the caves, saying he had been moved to new stables, but on no account to say where.

Holmes sent Lestrade a wire, asking him to liaise with the local police, requesting them to keep a lookout stationed on Grimpen moor.

My notes are a bit hazy but I remember full well that Sir Henry was happy to see us depart. Holmes warned him, and not for the first time, that Stapleton was a master at assuming many disguises, and could even have rivalled Sir Henry Irving when it came to the business of adopting a role and giving the character credibility.

CHAPTER EIGHTEEN

On arriving back at Baker Street we found that the letter from Sir Giles Hipkiss that Holmes had been expecting had been delivered by a private messenger. Hipkiss, Holmes said, was taking no risks, but why, for he had no idea of what Holmes had in mind?

On the journey home the train had been held up for over twenty minutes whilst a herd of cows was cleared off the line. It was during this period that Holmes gave me a potted biography of Hipkiss, who had been in his year at Winchester. To begin with, Hipkiss, who had a Black Country accent, was not accepted. He was mimicked, derided and on several occasions when playing rugby was physically attacked. Hipkiss, who had the backbone and grit of his forbears, bore all this with fortitude. His grandfather and father, through hard work allied to superior intelligence, had dragged themselves out of the mire, eventually owning their own mine and within a decade taking over two more in the district.

Holmes, who had joined Hipkiss in the school archery sessions was also derided for taking the part of an outsider, but as a boy Giles showed all the fortitude and courage of his ancestors and within months had been accepted. He did, however, have the last laugh by turning the tables and finishing his final year as head boy.

During the journey it became quite obvious to me that Holmes was telling me about the Director's background in order to convince himself that Hipkiss still possessed sufficient backbone to become involved with men who could be tried and hanged for high treason. The letter suggested 10 o'clock the following morning.

As we walked into a palatial office, Sir Giles rose to greet us and asked Holmes what had taken him so long.

My friend was quite taken aback. 'Are you saying that you were expecting me?'

'Of course, man! The message was loud and clear. When one of the guards was checking offices on the first floor he found your brother's office door wide open. For no apparent reason he elected to go through coat pockets and found, quite by chance, three pages on new methods to deal with fingerprinting. I have no intention, Holmes, of asking you to name who was responsible for this legerdemain. All I can say is that it was an excellent idea but not necessary because within days I was about to enlist your help.'

'Help, Hipkiss, in what way?' My friend, I have to admit, looked puzzled.

'We both know that Mycroft would never have been involved in demonstrations and anarchic riots against the crown and as for burning the Ripper papers, that was an act to protect the monarchy.'

'Those papers, according to my brother, must have been placed on his office desk while he was dining at the *Diogenes* club by someone who knew that he invariably worked into the small hours.'

'I realised that, Holmes, which is why I questioned Charles Boyce and his assistant Macey, as well as all the staff employed in the Record Office about the lapse of security. Boyce was unable to throw any light on the problem because at the time of Mycroft's arrest he was spending three days in Holland with his wife's father, who is an attaché at the Embassy in the Hague.'

'I have never been introduced to the gentleman,' said Holmes, 'but it is more than possible that I caught a glimpse of him entering the *Red Dragon* and leaving by the rear door. A tall, thin, fair-haired man with blue eyes; Germanic looking, but with an open countenance, followed by a middle-aged man of swarthy complexion, moustache, no beard, and wearing spectacles.

'Macey, that has to be Macey,' said Hipkiss emphatically, 'who serves as Boyce's right-hand man in the records department.'

'Do I understand, Hipkiss,' said Holmes, abruptly changing the subject, 'that you were in no way associated with the arrest of my brother?'

'I was associated but the decision to remove him was made at a high-level cabinet meeting, *sub rosa,* you understand, but my view on the matter was not accepted. Now that we have received information of a most serious uprising, some members of the original committee have suffered a *volte face.* Another reason for the change in climate has been due to the reports we have been receiving from Falconby and a diagnosis on the prisoner's state of mind from a Doctor Breucot, who says, without doubt, that Mycroft is innocent. We need your brother here to assess the situation in the capital before it is too late to prevent mayhem.'

Hipkiss was quite taken aback when Holmes explained that Mycroft was against attempts to reinstate him until the perpetrators of the plot had been apprehended and brought to justice.'

'Apprehended! Good God, man! How does he expect us to do that?'

'By infiltrating a cabal that operates under the aegis of the Hanover Club.'

'You are joking, Holmes!. The Hanover Club is Boyce's favourite hunting ground, and he is a man in whom I have implicit trust. You may have seen him leaving a public house by a back door but there would have been a very good reason for that. He is in total charge of records and a man in that position has to be above suspicion.'

'Hipkiss,' said Holmes slowly, 'would you be prepared to risk everything you have ever worked for, everything you have achieved, everything you hold dear if there were a chance of infiltrating the cabal, unravelling the conspiracy and saving the country from total disaster? I have to tell you that it is the only method that Mycroft can devise that would save the monarchy. He also feels that you should enlist the services of Falconby who, in the past, has used effective strategies in dealing with riots, never forgetting the example of *Bloody Sunday*.'

'That, I have to admit, has been at the back of my mind for some time,' he said whilst constantly tapping the desk with the bowl of his pipe. 'Are you suggesting, Holmes, that I join the Hanover Club?'

'Not you in particular, but Mycroft says that whoever has the stomach for the affair should join immediately. Be there tonight, and after having drunk too much, start carping about the state of the country, about a queen who is miserly and spends more time in Scotland than in the capital. All these remarks must be said when Boyce is within hearing distance.'

'Good God, man, you are saying that Boyce is involved?'

Holmes shrugged. 'How do I know? But the point does need to be proved one way or the other',

"In that case, Holmes, I suppose someone must join the club, if only to prove you wrong.'

Holmes glanced in my direction. It was quite evident that he considered the day lost. There was a knock at the door, a welcome relief from the tension that was building. A steward entered with a tray of coffee. After pouring three cups he left without a word being spoken.

While we sipped our coffee in silence Hipkiss wandered round the vast room, then, after staring through the window for several minutes, he returned to his desk and pulled out a sheaf of papers. Handing the top sheet to Holmes, he told him to cast his eyes over it.

Holmes was staggered. 'This is unbelievable. Surely we have a better system than this? It amounts to throwing a die in a game of chance.

'It is called democracy, Holmes. There were eleven of us who sat on the board at this high-powered cabinet meeting to decide Mycroft's fate. As you can see, five voted against arrest and five voted for incarceration. The Minister had the casting vote. It could have gone either way. Maybe your brother and the Minister had crossed swords in the past. Who knows? As you can see there are five who could join the Hanover. Would not that be the best way forward?'

'No!' Holmes was decisive. 'My brother said in the first instance only one man should join, otherwise plotters might imagine that they were under threat and go underground.'

'In that case I must be the one. No time like the present. I will apply for membership tonight.'

'Excellent!' cried Holmes and he made a resounding slap on the table. 'You have not changed over the years, still fearless and resolute.'

'No, Holmes, I am fearful, which is why I must grasp the nettle. Awful expression that, but you know what I mean.'

Holmes went on to explain that once Hipkiss felt that the cabal had taken him on board, then the next step would be to suggest a friend from Wales who had fought hard for Welsh supremacy. This so-called friend, he went on to explain, who was a practised wrestler and no mean boxer would be there as protection. Hipkiss relaxed noticeably when he realised he would not be alone.

'And from whence, Holmes, will this Welsh dragon come?'

'In your youth you may remember him as having been one of the three witches.'

'Three witches? Ah, I have it! You are alluding to the school play. We were two of the witches and Ponting was the third but he came from Norfolk and you, I believe, from Sussex. Of course,' he said as light dawned. 'You boxed, you wrestled and you were pretty nifty with a foil.'

'Yes, my achievements at school have always stood me in good stead. I shall come disguised as Glynn Williams, your Welsh friend. Fortunately I have a smattering of that inelegant language, can even sing their national anthem, adding much to the verisimilitude that an actor needs when stepping into the skin of an unusual character. We have no time to lose. No more than seven days.'

'You must not come here again, Holmes. Every day during the lunch hour I walk round St James Park. Tomorrow I will expect to meet this Welsh dragon but what will he look like? How will I recognise him?'

'A moustache, but no beard, spectacles and a broad brimmed hat to cast shadows over his face. A long brown coat to hide any armaments he may be carrying in an inside pocket. A green scarf decorated with a red dragon and wearing an artificial daffodil in his top button-hole.'

Hipkiss gave a deep throaty laugh. 'Do you know, Holmes, I am now looking forward to the challenge.'

CHAPTER NINETEEN

Having spent a couple of hours perfecting his disguise as a Welsh dragon Holmes managed to persuade Mrs Hudson to part with a green scarf. On it he drew a spectacular dragon before asking her if she could cut up one of his red ties in the shape of this legendary creature, then machine it firmly on to the green scarf. I have to say that she joined in the spirit of the charade by making a splendidly eye-catching addition to my friend's wardrobe. Also, without asking questions and with a twinkle in her eye, she filled a bag with stale bread intended for the colourful ducks on the lake in St James Park.

Leaving Baker Street just before twelve, we walked to Marylebone Road before hailing a cab. If one of our regulars had picked us up outside 221B it is possible that, despite my friend's brilliant disguise, he would have been able to recognise Holmes by his height and build. Alighting at the end of the Mall near Admiralty Arch, we took separate paths towards the lake. Holmes settled himself down on a bench while I wandered to the far side of the lake where I proceeded to feed the ducks, but at the same time keeping a look-out for anyone who might be following Hipkiss.

At a glance one could easily ascertain that Glynn Williams was a Welsh nationalist. The loose brown coat was more than adequate to hide any bulky items being carried in an inside pocket; the brown hat effectively hid his face, and the red dragon on a bright green background spoke volumes. There was not the slightest chance of Holmes being recognised. He had never failed when adopting a disguise, even fooled me time after time.

Within half an hour the two men were sitting on a bench, discussing progress. Hipkiss, fully aware that he was being watched, said that he had been accepted as a member of the Hanover, where he had already made considerable progress. Much to his dismay and anger, he had been left in no doubt that Boyce was the prime mover of the London cabal. The man even had the effrontery to ask him if he spoke German but despite having made the grade in languages Hipkiss denied all knowledge of the language. He knew full well, from the reaction of several members, who were euphoric when they realised that such an important personage had joined the ranks, that he had given them confidence. With such a man in their midst, how could the coup fail?

From my viewpoint across the lake I could see that Hipkiss was under surveillance. One apparent tramp, lying on the grass beyond the bench, was being ordered to get off the grass by a park-keeper. That man swore at the keeper and staggered his way out of the park but another fellow was sitting on a nearby bench, reading a paper. From time to time he peered at me. Not wanting to look involved in the action, I jettisoned the last piece of bread to the ducks before making my way out of the park.

The gambit worked, for once again he got stuck behind the newspaper, totally ignoring me. As I meandered towards Constitution Hill I spotted a small middle-aged man of swarthy complexion who was limping badly, making his way towards Hipkiss. Just before reaching the bench he stopped suddenly, as if his leg was giving him a sharp pain but it was quite obvious when he bent down that the pain had been caused by a stone in his shoe. Holmes, immediately recognising him as Macey, one of the men he had seen leaving the *Red Dragon,* was suddenly inspired. He excelled himself by ranting about the plight of poor families living in the Welsh valleys before standing up and singing *Land of my Fathers.* I was expecting the park keeper to ask him to move on but he just stood and applauded. I can only assume he was of Welsh extraction. The man, having put his shoe back on, apologised to Hipkiss for intruding during the lunch period.

Holmes told me later that it was Macey from the Record Office who had the gall to ask his lord and master whether he had given any thought to introducing a Welsh patriot to the Hanover. Holmes said Hipkiss, distinctly annoyed that one of the lower echelons should address him directly, told the man to get back to the office immediately. He would consider the proposition later that day after discussing the matter with Boyce.

Even from where I stood, I could see that Macey was grinning to himself as he wended his way back to the office. No doubt Boyce had given him a brief to keep track of the Director. It was obvious to Holmes that Hipkiss had not fully realised that he was placing himself in the hands of many dubious characters who, if the coup failed, could well implicate him.

Despite the fact that the break-through had been achieved, Holmes returned to Baker Street in very low spirits. It was a case of first the cocaine, then continuous Schubert, until I could stand it no longer.

'What is the matter with you, Holmes? This is the depressive state I expect to see when you have nothing to occupy you and no cases to solve. Now you have two investigations on hand and you are in a far worse state then usual.'

'You are right, as usual, Doctor, when you say I am in a parlous state. On the one hand I am torn between tracking down Stapleton, a malefactor of the first order, whom I allowed to escape, and on the other hand, saving my brother's reputation by following his dictum in order to prevent an uprising. Priorities, Watson! Saving the monarchy, should without doubt, be the most important issue but owing to my stupidity Sir Henry is the target for a man who has murder in mind. If Stapleton succeeds I will have the business on my conscience for the rest of my life.'

Before I had time to suggest a remedy other than cocaine we heard Mrs Hudson ascending the stairs. 'Come in,' shouted Holmes, 'do not stand on ceremony.'

Smiling, she wished us both good evening, then handed Holmes a letter that had just arrived by the afternoon post. 'When you have had time to read the letter, sir, that Mr Evans is here again. Says the matter is urgent.'

'Then do not keep him waiting, Mrs Hudson, send him straight up.'

Without waiting for her to close the door, he skimmed through the missive, then, with a triumphant smile, handed it to me. The letter from Falconby, I have to say, proved to be a better remedy than any medicine.

Dear Homer,

Baines and Smith have visited every school in Bristol and outlying districts. Only two new teachers have been appointed during the past six weeks. Flancey who is in his

217

early thirties, is now teaching at the Cathedral School and Vandeleur, a man probably in his late thirties or early forties, is teaching mathematics and natural history at the Grammar School. Both Baines and Smith have been discreet by not making a direct approach to schools. They have obtained information by chatting to local innkeepers and the few parents waiting to meet children after school.

A word of warning. School holidays commence after the prize giving in a week's time.

My mother is improving! You will be pleased to learn that I have an appointment with the Minister at the Home Office in the morning. Your brother was right, time is not on our side, Homer. Would prefer to talk direct but better, I thought, not to make direct contact with you.

From your old sparring partner.'

I found it hard to believe that Stapleton had been stupid enough to use the name Vandeleur again, but Holmes disagreed.

'It was a question of time, Watson. He needed foolproof references detailing his achievements in York as a headmaster, as well as copies of the accolades he received on his outstanding work as a naturalist. He knows he will hang, but that is unimportant when compared with one overriding ambition concerning his son.'

'Holmes, if young Arthur inherits a tainted title he will eventually realise that his position in society is unacceptable because it was assumed through the act of a criminal father.'

'Yes, that is the truth of the matter, but now we have only seven days left in which to take Vandeleur before the school term ends. No time for philosophising, only time for a pragmatic and reasoned plan of action. We need to discuss the matter with Lestrade'

We heard Evans making a slow climb up the stairs. After a hard day's graft his war injury probably gave him a great deal of pain. I opened the door for him and told him to take the weight off his feet. He looked a little dazed but nevertheless sat down.

'Mr Holmes, sir,' he whispered tearfully, 'I have terrible news, never thought things would get this far.'

'What things, Evans?'

'It is just too awful, sir, too awful for words. Sniffy Taylor is....is dead.'

'Dead!' Holmes looked at me in total disbelief. 'Are you saying', he asked clenching and unclenching his fists, 'that he was murdered?'

Evans burst into tears. It was a sad sight to see a man who had been so confident reduced to such an abject state. Holmes poured him a brandy which I persuaded him to drink.

'Holmes, he is suffering from shock. As soon as we have heard what actually happened I will call a cab and take him home. He needs a good night's sleep.'

Holmes, sitting beside him, said softly, 'You had better tell us what occurred, but take your time.'

'He was killed early yesterday evening, sir, possibly about seven o'clock but I can't tell you the exact time. He was found dead in the street outside the Northumberland Hotel.'

'Any idea what he was doing?'

Evans shook his head. 'He talked a lot, as you know, but he had never mentioned the hotel. It was always the *Red Dragon* or the *Hanover Club*. You do see what it means, Mr Holmes, if they was on to Sniffy then they could be on .....'

'You have nothing to fear.'

'My wife is frightened, she didn't want me to come here.'

'Of course she is,' said Holmes, 'but you have nothing to be scared about. You have always been most circumspect in your visits.'

'But I hid those papers.....'

'The Director has not the slightest desire to know who was courageous enough to plant the papers in my brother's coat.'

Evans breathed a sigh of relief.'

'Now what else do you know about Taylor?'

'He was seen by one of his mates leaving the building soon after six, carrying his old canvas bag, but I heard that when they found him an hour or so later the bag was missing.'

'How do you know this?'

'A copper came to the offices and asked the porters where Sniffy lived so that they could let his family know.'

'But how did the police know where he was employed?'

'I reckon they must have picked him up before, after he had one too many.'

'Could be! Could be! Watson, after you have taken Evans home, would you be good enough to call at the Yard and leave a message for Lestrade, asking him to get in touch with me as soon as possible to discuss an urgent matter? Later tonight I have to put in an appearance at the Hanover as well as planning a method of entrapping a schoolteacher in Bristol.'

It was nine o'clock before Lestrade appeared, leaving very little time for Holmes to discuss the Bristol business and the demise of Sniffy Taylor.

Lestrade could tell us very little about the incident. He had been called to the Northumberland Hotel by the manager, who was irate about the number of visitors who had been approached by beggars, and to exacerbate matters a beggar had the gall to get murdered. Lestrade was only too pleased to inform that odious man that Taylor had been employed at the Home Office as a messenger.

The only witness to the incident was a hotel doorman, who was assisting a guest with his luggage when he caught a brief glimpse of Sniffy handing over a package to a guest who immediately entered the hotel. He saw a man run after Sniffy as he was walking away, but was unaware that Sniffy had been knifed in the back and his bag grabbed. All Lestrade could tell us was that the unidentifiable assailant had made a quick getaway and that he had made no headway in tracing the guest who accepted the package.

Holmes had not much time to enlighten Lestrade about Sniffy's dubious visits to the Hanover. He did, however, make it clear that they were part of a much more serious problem affecting the country, but of immediate concern was a venture that could wait no longer.

Lestrade was flabbergasted when he learnt that Stapleton, now known as Vandeleur, was teaching in Bristol.

'Then, Holmes, we must pick him up at once.'

'No, Lestrade, this man is a highly perceptive creature. At the slightest smell he would once again evade capture. We must outmanoeuvre him. The strategy I have in mind is the only way.'

For a few moments Lestrade absorbed those few words, then, with a half-smile on his face, said, 'Let's be having it then!'

Holmes' strategy, I have to say, sounded effective but would it end in checkmate?

'Grammar Schools,' said Holmes, 'always have an end of the year prize-giving ceremony. Bristol will be no different from every other major city. It invariably happens on the penultimate day of the summer term, leaving you six days in which to organise local forces, but I have great faith in you, Inspector. I know you can do it. I suggest that you travel down with me tomorrow on the early morning express.'

'An excellent suggestion, Mr Holmes. The Bristol constabulary may not measure up to our London chaps but I know I can rely on the fellows in plain clothes. That rogue will not escape me a second time.'

'Then, my dear fellow, we will travel down by the first train in the morning to enlist the help of the headmaster. You will not recognise me, garbed in the role of a parent whose son is not making the grade, but it is necessary subterfuge, otherwise the whole enterprise could founder. The name of Sherlock Holmes must not even be whispered to your colleagues. During prize-giving all the masters will be in attendance. The hall will be full of scholars and doting parents, eager to see their progeny being awarded for their proficiency either in sport or in more brain-testing examinations. In a week's time your men will mingle with parents entering the hall but it is imperative that they select end seats near the exits. Once the doors have been closed and the school song is being sung, more men will take up positions outside all exits to the hall and those leading from the platform.

We have to remember that neither you nor your men have ever seen Stapleton, but he is a past master of disguise and even I could be fooled. To make sure all your men recognise Stapleton who, as you know, is now calling himself Vandeleur, I will ask the Headmaster to make a special announcement before his final speech.

During the course of this announcement he will gesture in Vandeleur's direction, praising him for the way in which he has managed, in such a short time, to guide the 6th Form fencing team to a major inter-schools victory. He will ask him to accept an award in this connection, but Vandeleur, who is no fool, will realise he has been rumbled and will make for the nearest exit, which may be at the back of the platform. Not knowing the hall, I cannot be specific. The men guarding platform exits will not have set eyes on Vandeleur but they must apprehend anyone who rushes off the platform.

'Leave it to me, Holmes. I will have every exit covered. That man will hang before the month is out.'

I have no doubt that Lestrade could see himself gaining the plaudits, but where would Holmes be without such a man to do his bidding? To my disappointment, Holmes asked me to remain in town. Apart from the fact that Vandeleur would recognise me, which was true, he said that I was the linchpin in the destruction of the pernicious and deadly cabal. He told me to make sure that I lunch at the Northumberland Hotel the following day, talk to the receptionist and say that I was expecting to meet Herr Bach, an old friend of mine, but was disappointed because he had failed to show up. In that way, Holmes said, it should be easy enough to ask whether there were any other Germans staying.

Once that had been established, Holmes suggested that I have words with the doormen and ask whether either of them had been on duty the evening Sniffy was killed. If so, despite the fact that the whole episode happened so quickly, could the man on duty describe the height, build and the apparel of the guest who entered the hotel prior to the murder? Lestrade said that he too would be interested in any snippets of information gleaned from the hotel staff.

The Inspector left after less than half an hour's discussion. A man with a purpose, a man who, like Holmes, was determined to get his man.

I always hate missing the action. Remaining in London while Holmes was involved in trapping Stapleton was anathema. However, Holmes was right. Stapleton would recognise me and all the carefully laid plans would prove useless, but I believed that my friend, a rare occurrence for him, had not given enough thought to matters relating to the hotel.

'Holmes,' I suggested soon after Lestrade's departure, 'tomorrow could be too late. Why don't I visit the Northumberland tonight?'

'An excellent idea,' said Holmes clapping his hands and taking me by surprise. 'You may well find the same doorman and the same receptionists on duty. Why did I not think of that?'

Within half an hour I was in the hotel foyer, having left Holmes with time enough to perfect his appearance as Glynn Williams. He decided not to hail a cab outside the house, safer to walk to Marylebone Road. Cab-drivers were observant, they lived their lives through the passengers they carried. No need to take risks.

The doorman at the hotel, who had seen Sniffy Taylor handing over a package to one of the guests, was of little assistance. All he had seen was the back of a man about six foot in height, entering the hotel.

For a time I sat in the lounge reading *The Evening News*, or at least appearing to be reading the paper. All of the fellows, several of them with their wives, appeared harmless enough but the successful spy must be one of the crowd, never drawing attention to himself. After dining, and before returning to Baker Street, I chatted to the receptionist, explaining that my evening had been a total waste of time because my German friend, Herr Bach, had not arrived as expected. The receptionist, a sympathetic man, looked through the list of guests.

'No mention of a Herr Bach, sir, but there is a German gentleman who has been here for three days.'

'Maybe I know him?'

'Herr Hessler, sir, does the name ring a bell?'

'No I am afraid not.' I thanked him and left the hotel to wander along the embankment, wondering how Holmes and Hipkiss were faring.

Holmes arrived at the Hanover fifteen minutes before the meeting was due to start. Hipkiss, who was already there, introduced the Welshman to Boyce and two other fellows who also worked in the Home Office. There was no need for Holmes to be introduced to the swarthy-faced man, whom he knew to be Macey. Apart from Macey there were at least four conspirators from within the government, all of whom had signed an oath of allegiance to the Crown.

Hipkiss, in a whisper, told Holmes that Falconby was now back with his old regiment, on a temporary basis. The Minister had agreed that expediency in tackling the threat head-on was the only way to save the monarchy.

Five minutes before the meeting opened, Holmes, hardly able to believe his eyes, stared at a tall, thin, blond-haired man who had just entered the lounge. A man he last saw through a miasma of tobacco smoke in the *Red Dragon*, whose clothes were obviously tailored in Germany and whose password was *a dram of Hock*.

Ignoring everyone, the stranger made straight for Boyce and speaking in German, asked him if everyone was present. Neither Hipkiss nor Holmes gave any sign that they could understand what was being said. The German, whose name was Gunter Hessler, the very man who was in residence at the Northumberland Hotel, told Boyce that the Kaiser had not been informed about the plan to storm Buckingham Palace because it was generally thought that he might object to the means being used to gain the empire he coveted. Hessler went on to say that the Kaiser would be taken by surprise, a genuine reaction quite obvious to the onlookers, but the joyous surprise would lead to the fulfilment of an ambition.

A few minutes later Boyce asked the stewards to lock all doors, before asking the thirteen men present to sit down while he went through the next stage of the operation in detail. First of all, Holmes had told me with a smile, he introduced a new member, describing him as an ardent Welsh nationalist, an announcement that was applauded. The men seated themselves with Hipkiss and Holmes sitting on opposite sides of the room, giving them a chance to watch the reactions of those close to them.

Boyce then introduced Gunter Hessler, not his real name, he had said, amidst much laughter. To Holmes the ingenious plan Boyce unveiled had all the hallmarks of Professor Moriarty stamped all over it.

The thirteen men were all given the names and addresses of twenty-two disreputable scoundrels who had all spent time in Wormwood Scrubs or Wandsworth Gaol. Hessler made it clear that all these ruffians were to be contacted immediately after the meeting and during the early hours of the morning. While the conspirators were delivering the instructions they were advised to keep their hats well down over their faces, not enter any houses and remain in the shadows. The thugs, who were expecting to be approached, knew that they would be well-paid for their nefarious activities, but not until the deed was done. What they did not know, however, was that if the plot misfired they would take the blame.

At that juncture Hessler stood up, thanked the men for their devotion to the Kaiser's cause, then went on to explain that on the sheet of paper they had been given, positions were clearly marked, with foolproof instructions for each man. Stationed at many points along the route, points including Admiralty Arch, Constitution Hill, Queen's Walk, Spur Road and St James's Park, there would be two men carrying out precise instructions, but first they had to keep their eyes on the approach to Buckingham Palace. When the Kaiser's coach was halfway down the Mall, Hessler would raise a white triangular flag. The men on Constitution Hill would immediately begin shouting *Down with the Monarchy*. Those as far away as the Admiralty Arch might have difficulty in seeing the flag, but on hearing the shouting they were to join in the mêlée by cheering the Kaiser. At the moment the flag was raised, one of the best shots in the German Army would kill two of the guards standing by the open gates to the Palace, giving access to the vast courtyard.

As soon as this had been achieved the men leading the riot at the west end of the Mall would be given orders to drive the crowd into the courtyard. Hessler told the assembled men that a shot at the Queen while she was standing on the balcony had been discussed but this was thought to be unproductive because it was entirely possible that the crowd might suddenly feel sympathy for the woman, thereby undoing the carefully structured plans.

Holmes and Hipkiss were each given the addresses of men in the East End. Holmes told me that while peering closely at his instructions in the pretence that he was short-sighted he was able to read much of what had been written on the

228

papers held by the men sitting on both sides of him. One had addresses in Balham and Tooting and on the other side there were addresses in Clapham. It seems the net was widespread.

Hessler asked his audience if there were any questions and after answering a few queries he handed over to Boyce, who made the surprise announcement of the evening. The final meeting of the conspirators would take place at Ascot, the home of racing, the day after tomorrow.

Hipkiss laughed out loud. 'The day after tomorrow, Boyce! You must be joking.'

'No, Sir Giles, I have never been more serious. The meeting will give me a chance to confirm that you have all managed to contact the rabble-rousers. We can't leave a stone unturned, so let us drink to the success of our final meeting at Ascot on the day of the Queen's Handicap Chase.'

Members stood on their feet, laughing about the choice of race, and drank to the success of the event. Once the laughter had subsided, the men all settled down again, while one of the waiters went round the room handing each man a ticket for Ascot. They were all ordered to meet thirty minutes before the first race in a marquee covered in Union Jacks.

On leaving the meeting Holmes and Hipkiss hailed a cab, and gave audible instructions to the cabbie to take them to Petticoat Lane, but once out of sight of the club they turned west instead of east to Hipkiss's house in Belgrave Square. All was quiet when they entered, Lady Hipkiss and the servants all safely in bed.

Hipkiss thought it the most chilling and saddest day of his life to see four trusted men from the Home Office involved in high treason. Holmes was more phlegmatic, said it had happened before, and no doubt would happen again. Hipkiss hid both sheets of instructions, never to be delivered, in a secret drawer in the davenport. They would be needed, in the future, by the prosecutor when the traitors were arraigned for high treason.

Hipkiss was all for calling on the services of Falconby and Lestrade by arresting all the men who were present at the Hanover. Holmes advised Sir Giles against such premature action because the men could deny any intent, saying it was a great game played out to fool Sir Giles. They had to hold their horses until after the meeting at Ascot.

After a circuitous journey, Holmes, after making sure he was unobserved, called on Falconby to give him a blow-by-blow account of what had happened at the Hanover, thus giving him time to marshal his forces.

Finally both men agreed that Hipkiss should be kept in the dark. Better for him to be amazed and bewildered by the operation Falconby had in mind. A man's nervousness and stance could signal that the last move was about to be played out, thereby warning the black king and his conspirators to be on their guard. Total surprise was a tactic that Falconby had successfully used many times.

'Enjoy the Queen's Handicap Chase, Holmes. We have to win,' he said quietly as Holmes left quietly by the back door into the darkest night.

Holmes then journeyed to Lestrade's home in the East End. Much to his chagrin, the change of plans meant that he and the inspector would have to delay their journey to Bristol until all the conspirators had been apprehended, but no matter what happened Holmes had made up his mind that he would attend the prize-giving. Lestrade, who was of like-mind, maintained that with Falconby in charge of the Ascot operation they would complete both missions.

Holmes arrived back at Baker Street at two in the morning, having changed his carefully orchestrated plans. He roused me from my slumbers and asked me to make notes of everything that had taken place before any of the fine detail became so deeply buried in his subconscious that it could be years before he brought it back to mind.

CHAPTER TWENTY

Mrs Hudson, who was surprised to see us both up and dressed at a respectable hour, was totally taken aback when she learned that we would both be spending the day at the races.

Holmes refused to eat a morsel of food, but sat smoking that infernal shag tobacco while I put away a good breakfast. We discussed the *modus operandi* on the day that Mycroft could well be enjoying the last of his cigars. In my view divine intervention was needed, but Holmes had more faith in Falconby and Lestrade than in the supernatural.

'You could say, Watson, that this is the eleventh hour. Neither Hipkiss nor I have any idea how Boyce will be playing his hand. The order of the day, we were told, is to behave like race-goers, and between races, make occasional visits to a marquee decked overall with Union Jacks.'

'Well, Holmes, take his advice and behave like a race-goer. Since you have nothing to occupy you other than surmise we could study form on the journey down to Ascot.'

'We could, Watson, though not together, but why do you need my help? You know a great deal about racing.'

'I should do. As you know, I pay for it with half my war wound pension.'

'On no account must you be seen conversing with a Welsh nationalist. Take the binoculars and keep me and the participants in this drama in your sights, for in the future you may be needed as a witness.'

I have to admit that I was afraid for Holmes. The thirteen men involved were being controlled by Moriarty, who had no qualms about disposing of anyone who crossed his path. Holmes would be a prime target.

We travelled on the same train, but two carriages apart. I scanned through the runners listed in the *Racing News* but found it hard to concentrate. It did not really matter whether *Royal Faction* came in at ten to one or *Lifelong* at six to one. All that mattered was that Holmes and Hipkiss won their bet and were ahead of the field.

Although it seemed like the work of a madman to arrange the final meeting for the conspirators at an event attended by thousands of race-goers, Holmes thought otherwise, saying that it would be eminently workable. By the time we reached Ascot I had chosen only two horses that, after studying form, I considered were worth backing. *Verity* at twelve to one in the 2 o'clock and *Victory Boy*, an outsider at thirty-three to one in the 2.45, but was that tempting providence?

On alighting at Ascot, Holmes, ignoring me, climbed on board a coach running a relay service to the course. I shared a cab with three other enthusiasts who were certain that they had backed the right horse in the *Queen's Handicap Chase*.

Holmes was able to enter the hallowed turf by using the special guest ticket he had been given but I had to queue to purchase mine. 'Behave naturally,' Holmes had said so I laid out money on *Verity* and *Victory Boy*, a florin each way on both, never for a moment expecting any winnings.

As I climbed the steps into the main stand I caught a glimpse of Hipkiss talking to Boyce. It looked such an innocent encounter – they could have been discussing office business. Despite the fact that the flag-covered marquee was some distance away it was easy, with the aid of the binoculars, to see men drifting in and out. No women were allowed inside the marquee.

At a quarter to two the business of the afternoon began, with an excellent marine band playing the National Anthem, followed by some rousing Handelian tunes. Shortly before the 2 o'clock I noticed several men emerging from the marquee before making their way to the side of the course.

Holmes told me later that there were always two men on guard, stationed just inside the entrance to the marquee, not visible to the public outside. Anyone not able to produce a guest ticket never crossed the threshold. From my vantage point in the stand I had not even caught a glimpse of the men. Inside the marquee there were two waiters, offering a goodly selection of sandwiches, as well as wine to suit all palates. Holmes found a large drawing tacked on to an easel more interesting than the sustenance. The rough charcoal drawing outlined the course, the stand, the stables, the paddock and the exits. No one, other than Hipkiss and Holmes, showed any interest in the very loosely drawn plan.

For a time, I have to admit, the racing actually absorbed me. *Verity* running in the 2 o'clock came in a close fourth. Was that, I wondered, to be the story of the afternoon but no, my luck changed. *Victory Boy* was beaten into second place by only a nose but at least I made a profit on my investment. I have to admit that at the time, I thought that being beaten into second place by such a short distance was an omen. The next race, the *Queen's Handicap Chase* 3.45, was the main event of the afternoon. The crowd converged on the betting booths, forming enormous queues. It was during the period prior to and during the 3.45 race that momentous plans were being hatched.

Those planning the final meeting knew that everyone on the ground would be concerned with the main race, therefore it would be a perfect time and place, infinitely safer than meeting at night in chambers, where comings and goings could be observed. The flap to the marquee was now closed to everyone apart from the guards, who were sitting on the grass eating sandwiches and drinking what I took to be ale. To an onlooker they were race-goers who had lost all their money and were no longer interested in seeing the final race. Inside there was a hush as Boyce removed the tacks holding the sketch of the grounds in place, and in turning it over he revealed an extraordinarily detailed pen and ink drawing of Buckingham Palace, the nearby parks and adjoining roads.

Hessler, who was once again in evidence, joined Boyce in repeating all the directions the cabal had been given at the Hanover. Only one man queried the contradiction in the move to rid of the country of a queen only to supplant her with the Kaiser, a German king.

Boyce gave a deep, throaty laugh, telling the assembled men that the Kaiser might dream of taking over the British Empire but that the British would never accept another Hanoverian monarch – the Kaiser would never rule. Hessler, according to Holmes, looked quite taken aback but quickly regained his composure and intimated that it was better to let events take their course, for who knew what would happen after the State Visit?

At the end of the meeting Hessler reminded his audience that on the day of the state visit mayhem would commence the moment he raised the white triangular flag. He then attempted to thank the plotters for their support but his words were drowned by the roar of the crowd as the *Queen's Handicap Chase* finished in a victory for *Cicero*, a horse I hadn't even considered to be in the running.

Fifteen minutes before the 3.45 commenced, the marine bandsmen, unnoticed by the crowd, were making their way towards the marquee, but without their musical instruments. The instruments had been exchanged for heavy arms. Ahead of them were a few of Lestrade's men, making straight for the opening flaps to the marquee. In a matter of seconds they had dragged the two guards, who were still sitting on the grass, well away from the scene of the action.

The bandsmen, standing to attention, surrounded the marquee. Only then did Falconby, accompanied by a bugler, approach the men, giving them a sign to remain stationary. I have to say that it was a splendid heart-warming sight. I prayed, fervently, for the strategy to succeed.

As the unsuspecting men in the marquee were preparing to leave, Boyce folded the map before handing it to one of the waiters, who placed it in a box containing empty bottles. Holmes, in a nonchalant manner, threw a cigar butt into the box. Then Hipkiss tore up his betting slip, adding that to the debris. Two more items for the prosecution, providing they were able to keep track of the box. The other waiter had a few words with Boyce, who, looking well satisfied with events, nodded and gave the man a heavy pat on the back. An accolade for work well done, but he was premature.

As the tent flaps were opened the bugle sounded loud and clear, causing many race-goers who were in the vicinity, and on their way to collect their winnings, to stop in their tracks. Lestrade and a veritable army of constables set about keeping the crowd at bay, making sure that no one came within fifty yards of the marquee.

At precisely 3.55 Falconby had given orders for the bugler to give the signal for action. Holmes said the piercing sound sent shivers down his back, a thrilling sound, but not to the men in the marquee, who up to that moment had been so confident. They were now utterly panic-stricken. Boyce, pulling out a revolver, swore at Hipkiss, saying that he had been responsible for this assault, but Hipkiss, who had no knowledge of the raid, looked so utterly stunned that Boyce knew he was not putting on an act. Holmes had saved the life of the Director by not warning him about the assault.

The Major in charge of the action entered the marquee with three of his men. Only Macey and Boyce were carrying revolvers, no doubt the rest of the conspirators had seen no reason why they should arrive at Ascot fully armed. Macey shot at one of the guards, hitting him in the chest but the guard, before collapsing, returned the fire, killing Macey instantly. During this incident Boyce made a sudden dive, attempting to crawl out from under the canvas, but Holmes put his foot firmly on the blackguard's back.

The cacophony created by the men shouting amidst the orders being yelled by the sergeant, meant that Holmes was able to gesture to Hipkiss to come and join him and stand with his back to the entrance. As expected, all the conspirators were keeping their eyes on the guards, fearful of being shot. Falconby had made it clear to the marines that there would be two men in the marquee, two tall men who would keep their backs to the action. These men were not to be arrested. Only when all the conspirators had been shackled could those two men walk free. Holmes and Hipkiss watched as Boyce, still lying on his stomach and held down by a heavy boot, was suddenly dragged out of the marquee by two invisible marines. They heard him screaming diabolical oaths as he was handcuffed before being led away.

From my vantage point I watched as the injured guard, who thankfully survived, was carried on a stretcher to a waiting ambulance. Eleven men in shackles were then led away, giving the large crowd a dramatic end to their afternoon's racing. Boyce, still shouting, was the first to be shoved into a police van and lastly, the corpse of Macey, wrapped in an old sheet, was carried, not too gently I have to add, to a van on the far side of the marquee out of my vision.

From where I stood it had been possible to see the final stages of what I thought was Holmes's greatest venture, but he didn't see it in that light. He now had only one thought in his mind and that was the return to Baskerville Hall.

Hipkiss made it clear that Holmes had been instrumental in Falconby's *coup de grâce,* thus saving Mycroft's reputation and the country he loved from being ravaged by a German invader.

CHAPTER TWENTY ONE

I woke to find Holmes pummelling me.

'What's the matter, Holmes?'

'We have to catch the early train and you have overslept.'

'Have you had any sleep at all?'

'An hour or so, but I now know why Sniffy was killed. He did, indeed, hand a package to Hessler leaving no doubt in my mind that it was his last job as a messenger which is why he met his quietus immediately after the task had been completed.'

Deciding that the time was not ripe for discussion. I rose and made some coffee, knowing there would be no need to disturb Mrs Hudson. Black coffee would sustain us until we could get breakfast on the train.

'Watson, ' said Holmes, as we made our way to Paddington, 'you have been a tower of strength and I have to say that at times your very silence has been the most comforting gift you can bestow.'

It was clear to me that deep down Holmes believed Stapleton would once again evade arrest, which is why, on the journey down, he was distinctly edgy. He knew there was no way to trap Stapleton unless he had the whole-hearted support of the headmaster, Geoffrey Charding, who had no idea that he was about to meet the greatest consulting detective in Europe. Would he, I wondered, be impressed?

Whilst I enjoyed an excellent breakfast, my friend took no more than half a dozen mouthfuls. During the meal Holmes mentioned that the very whisper of his name could jeopardize our position, he was too famous, too well-known. So it happened that when we arrived at the school I gave my name to the clerk, explaining that my brother would keep me company. The man gave us a cursory glance before asking us to follow him to the ante-room, where we could wait until the headmaster Mr Charding was free. In fact, five minutes later we were sitting comfortably in the Head's study.

Charding was a well-built Welshman with a deep, melodious voice. What was in the air in that country that produced so many teachers, policemen, clergymen and choristers? Even the women were migrating and taking up nursing in many hospitals across the length and breadth of England.

Charding was overjoyed to meet Holmes, but was appalled when he learnt how wrong he had been in his estimate of Stapleton. The papers in the name of Vandeleur had convinced him that the applicant was the right man for the job. He looked relieved when he realised that Falconby too had been fooled.

'Well, Mr Holmes, you must spell it out, tell me exactly how you plan to trap Vandeleur, and in the event will you need my help?'

'We cannot possibly take him without your assistance. The plan I have in mind has been given a seal of approval by Inspector Lestrade of Scotland Yard. He will already have taken a look at the hall in which your annual prize giving takes place, and made a note of all the exits. Several of his men will mingle with parents entering the hall. They will take up positions on end seats nearest to the exits. Once the doors have been closed more officers will take up positions outside the doors.'

'There are two stage exits, Mr Holmes.'

'They will have been noted, but unfortunately the Inspector will only have men outside those doors, which means they will never have set eyes on Vandeleur. However, to prevent the man escaping again they will have been given orders to apprehend anyone rushing from the platform after the prize giving commences.'

'How will the police in the hall know which of the masters on the platform is Vandeleur?'

'That, Mr Charding, is where we need your help. Presumably you make a final speech?' Charding nodded. 'In that case, could you make a prior announcement, extolling the virtues of Vandeleur's masterful teaching methods, utilised in the short time he has been in the school, especially his spectacular prowess with regard to the celebrated achievements of the 6th Form Fencing team and whilst doing so, gesture in his direction and prevail upon him to accept an award in this connection?'

'This means,' said Charding with the ghost of a smile, 'that all the officers in the hall will recognise him.'

'Holmes,' I said, thinking of the chaos that could be caused. 'He may not make a run for it which means the officers will have to arrest him on the platform.'

'Oh no, Watson. Vandeleur is a man who makes instant decisions. Just think about the way he killed the escaping convict and then that wretched clergyman on the train.'

'My pupils,' said Charding,' would enjoy the spectacle, but I have the feeling that both governors and parents would not be so enthralled.'

'I think your young scholars will be disappointed because he will make a dash for it. Now in my experience, a right-handed man standing on the right of the stage would make a quick dash for an exit on his right, but I would prefer him to use the exit on his left. This means, Doctor Charding, that when the masters join you on the platform I want Vandeleur to be seated on stage left – audience right, of course.'

'That will pose no problem, but why the left, Mr Holmes?'

'Because once through the exit he will be trapped in a long corridor with no access into the school grounds, whereas if he chose to go to his right he could possibly escape by dashing into the bushes on the far side of the entrance to the school.'

'You should be teaching geometry, Mr Holmes! Now is there anything else I can do for you?'

'Just one more request. Have you, by any chance, a bath-chair that could be placed at the end of the third row of chairs on the audience right?'

Charding frowned. 'A bath-chair! A bath-chair! Why yes, the caretaker's wife is disabled. I am sure we could borrow it for an afternoon.'

'But Holmes,' I exclaimed, 'why a bath-chair?'

'Because you, my friend, will become an invalid for a couple of hours, a distinguished-looking gentleman sporting a grey wig, thus preventing recognition.'

'With what object?' I asked.

'All will be explained, Watson but let us not detain Dr Charding a moment longer. We have to meet Lestrade in the cathedral to discuss the final moments of this drama.'

Lestrade was waiting for us in the Lady Chapel. Despite the fact that he had not slept since we last spoke the night before he was a live coil ready to spring. I had rarely seen him approach a case so enthusiastically. He laughed when Holmes told him I would be seated in a bath-chair - as a disabled man. No fear of Vandeleur recognising Dr Watson!

Two days later, as the school clock struck three, Dr Charding entered the hall, accompanied by the Chairman of the Governors. After they had been welcomed by resounding applause and cheers it was the turn of the masters to be feted, most of them entering with broad smiles on their faces. They remained standing while *God Save the Queen* was sung, followed by the school-song, which contained many references to the sea and its trade. As the men on the stage settled themselves down I took a quick glance at the masters sitting on the left, but failed to recognise Stapleton. Having seen him both as Stapleton and Henderson I had thought it would be relatively easy to pick out certain characteristics but I was wrong and kept my head down.

I would have enjoyed the occasion a great deal more had the situation not been so serious, but I appreciated the joy on the faces of the boys who made their way up on to the stage to receive cups or certificates of merit.

By a quarter past four the last prizes, medals for the 6th Form Fencing Team, had just been presented, and the Team exited stage right and down the steps to enthusiastic applause. Before making his final speech, Mr. Charding stated that he wished to make a special announcement. One of the newest members of staff, he said, had produced unbelievable academic results in the short time in which he had been with the school.

'But in particular,' said Mr. Charding ' I want to lavish praise on his superb tutelage of the 6th Form Fencing Team, guiding them, within a mere six weeks, to their recent elevation to Supreme Winners of the Inter-County Fencing Championships. In recognition of this prestigious achievement, it is my pleasure to present Mr. Vandeleur, as Senior Coach, with the Ceremonial Epee, traditionally awarded by the school since its inception, for outstanding achievement in the field of fencing.'

Vandeleur, now with a ginger moustache and longish auburn hair, was momentarily stunned but rapidly collected himself, and strode forward confidently to accept the accolade. The small, slightly-built First former who had been assisting all afternoon with the disbursement of prizes now moved forward, at a signal from the Headmaster, carrying the handsome, finely crafted foil, which nestled, gleaming, on a blue velvet cushion.

Vandeleur shook hands with Mr. Charding, lifted the foil and swept round swiftly to face his audience. His heels snapped smartly together as, with an expansive flourish, he held the blade aloft in salute, bowing his head stiffly in acknowledgement of the wave of applause which began to work its way through the assembled company.

Thronging the left-hand aisle, the 6th Form Fencing Team, in full regalia, broke into spontaneous applause. At the foot of the stage the Team captain beamed with pleasure and clapped enthusiastically. They were all unaware of the silent form who melted into their midst as the Hall erupted in a vast cacophony of sound. Hundreds of boys jumped up, clapping and cheering and stamping their feet.

Bang! All at once, directly behind me, a particularly enthusiastic pupil lost his footing, cannoning with some force into the back of my bath-chair, which then hurtled forward, at an angle, into the aisle. Putting out his hands to save himself, the unfortunate availed himself of a firm grip on a key element of my disguise: an iron-grey, somewhat distinguished-looking wig, which he then let go of in alarm and confusion, whereby it fell, disconsolately, to the floor.

Too late. Every muscle in Vandeleur's face hardened and his eyes locked with mine in a look of absolute, malevolent recognition. Several of Lestrade's men had risen uncertainly to their feet. Cobra-like, Vandeleur's left arm shot out, encircling the neck of the slender First former. Holding the blade to the child's neck, he began to drag the shocked and weeping boy along the stage towards the left exit. In the second row of the Hall, his mother fainted. For a few brief seconds nobody moved. The silence, punctuated only by the ragged sobbing of the boy, gave way to horrified gasps, screams and chaotic confusion.

Abruptly Vandeleur stopped. At the top of the stairs, blocking the stage left exit, epee drawn, was the 6th Form fencing captain, the favoured student of the master. Bonds of loyalty, respect and trust were shattered in this moment of utter betrayal. Vandeleur's face contorted into sheer studied contempt, as thrusting the captive child aside like a broken toy, he took up the challenge. Lestrade's men, standing but unsure, and mindful of the potential for innocent death, remained immobile.

It was over quickly. The youngster fought bravely but Vandeleur's superior skill was immediately evident, forcing the youth relentlessly down the steps and into the space in front of the stage. Suddenly the boy slipped and overbalanced violently. As he fell the foil spiralled out of his grip, hit the ground and spun some distance along the floor, its progress only arrested by the heel of a black boot emerging swiftly from amongst the ranks of the fencing team. Its owner deftly grasped the weapon, bowed, and with a theatrical flourish, saluted his opponent, the ghost of a smile playing about his lips.

Vandeleur roared. Every muscle in his face betrayed his visceral fear. Turning, he raced for the exit, as Holmes had predicted. Lestrade's men moved at last. Just as he reached the door my bath-chair, which I had furiously propelled forward in the confusion, caught the back of the escaping man's legs and succeeded in knocking him into the outstretched arms of two of Lestrade's men.

Holmes stood silently in the corridor smoking his pipe while Lestrade gave orders for the man to be handcuffed before being taken straight to Princeton, where he would be kept under close house arrest.

Vandeleur knew only too well, despite the disguise, that the pipe-smoking man was Holmes, which is why he spat at him and told him that this was not the end. Lestrade told him to shut his mouth because within a month he would be hanging from the gallows outside the prison, where the kids would be pelting him with rotten apples. The smile of satisfaction and relief on my friend's face made me realise what pressure he had been under for the past two years. From henceforth he knew that Baskerville was beyond the reach of an obsessive assassin, but would that satisfy him and cleanse him of guilt?

Holmes thanked Dr Charding for his assistance and apologised for disrupting the prize-giving ceremony but the Head believed that it was an event his boys would never forget, an unforgettable prize-giving in which Holmes, too, had gained the prize he had sought for two years.

Before returning to London we called at Baskerville Hall to inform Sir Henry that he no longer had to fear for his life. Beryl Stapleton was so overjoyed she surprised Holmes by jumping on a stool and kissing him on both cheeks. Arthur immediately clapped his hands and asked if he could now go out and fly his kite.'

'Yes,' yelled Baskerville, 'thanks to Mr Holmes that's exactly what we're all going to do!'

'Watson,' said Holmes, as the train pulled out, 'you can finish your notes tonight, but add a footnote to the effect that the church bells in Tavistock will ring out within a month, announcing Sir Henry Baskerville's marriage to a beautiful woman whose son will be accepted as heir to the vast estate.'

I had expected Holmes to be a little more relaxed on the return journey, but that was not the case. Something was still bothering him. 'What's getting to you, Holmes? Keeping it to yourself does you no good.'

'You are quite right, Doctor. All this could have been prevented had I pursued Stapleton on the moor two years since. Those poor souls at Baskerville Hall have been living on a knife edge.'

I said no more, but when we arrived at Baker Street everything changed. There on the table lay a letter, delivered, so Mrs Hudson said excitedly, from Downing Street. An invitation asking us both to dine with the Prime Minister the following evening.

'Now you can relax, Holmes. Enjoy the fruits of your labour and put these bugbears behind you.'

When we arrived at Downing Street we were surprised to find the Prime Minister, Falconby and Hipkiss, waiting for us, but there were six seats round the table and only five of us. Who, I wondered was late, who had the gall not to be on time for an invitation from the most important man in the country? 'Who,' I whispered to Holmes, 'ignores protocol?' Holmes, smiling to himself, put his fingers on his lips.

A waiter, appearing with a magnum of champagne, nodded at the Prime Minister, who immediately rose to his feet. 'Gentlemen,' he said, 'let us rise to welcome one of Her Majesty's most loyal servants.'

As we did as we had been bidden, Mycroft walked slowly into the room. It was every birthday and Christmas present I had ever received rolled into one. The brothers clasped hands and for the first time ever, I saw Holmes shed a few tears.

It was a dinner never to be forgotten, in which Holmes elaborated on every move he had made in his quest to trace Stapleton in order to solve the Baskerville mystery. He also outlined the moves that he had made in his efforts to clear his brother of unlawful arrest, which meant tracing the instigators of the plot whose intent was to dethrone Her Majesty. He paid tribute to both Lestrade and Falconby, knowing that without them his strategies would never have been successful. The Prime Minister, who was enthralled, said that the Queen, who was at Windsor, would want to hear the whole story first hand.

Before Holmes, who was now speechless, got his breath back, Mycroft made it quite clear that it was not the only purpose of the plot. His brother's reputation, he said, as the most prominent and successful consulting detective in Europe, could have been ruined by the pernicious Professor Moriarty had not Sherlock assumed the disguise of, Dr Breucot, an Austrian psychologist. Falconby stared open-mouthed at Holmes, never for one moment suspecting that he had adopted the mannerisms, clothes and appearance of the doctor who, shortly after he had visited the prison, had travelled to Dresden, intent on discovering when and where the demonstrations and riots in the capital would be taking place.

Before proposing a toast, Hipkiss said that both he and Mycroft owed their lives to an incredible detective. 'There is no doubt,' he said, 'that had I been warned of the assault by the marines in advance, Boyce would have shot me. I was saved by both ignorance and intelligence. An intelligent man, who together with Sir John, planned the raid and made sure that I remained in total ignorance. Gentlemen,' he said rising to his feet, 'let us drink to intelligence and ignorance – there is a place in this world for both.'